SAILING WITH HER WOLF

THE NIGHTSTAR SHIFTERS

ARIEL MARIE

"She is the gold at the end of the rainbow."

unknown

CHAPTER ONE

"Will your wolf like the ocean?" Zara's husky laugh filled her ear through the phone.

Marley Gerwulf smirked at her friend's question. She adjusted herself on her plush pillows on her bed as they discussed their upcoming trip of a lifetime. It was late, and they were both too excited. Marley glanced over at her clock on her nightstand, finding it a little past eleven at night. In a few days, they would leave for their adventure.

Marley had practically been raised on the water. Being a wolf shifter didn't mean they didn't like the water. Her pack, The Nightstar, was located on the coast of Southern California. Water was second nature to them. Her father, Evan Gerwulf, the alpha, had ensured Marley knew how to sail. He ran a boating company that was world renown. She had practically learned how to walk on her human and wolf legs on a boat.

"My wolf loves the ocean, silly." She chuckled. Her smile slowly disappeared as she thought about their plans. Three weeks at sea with her bestie would be amazing. Zara had just broken up with Bo, her cheating boyfriend, and it had been Marley's idea for them to get away. It had been a few months since Zara and Bo had separated, and Marley felt it was time to try to help her friend get over him.

What better way than a girls' trip on the ocean? Fresh air, open waters, and bright sun would do them both some good.

"And your father is okay with us taking one of his yachts out for a few weeks?"

"Of course." Marley rolled her eyes. She sighed, running her hand along her soft abdomen. She'd sailed plenty and held a license. This was not her first time taking a boat out into the ocean for a sailing trip.

"I'm just so excited. I'm so glad you thought of this. You always seem to know what will make me feel better," Zara replied softly.

Marley bit her lip at Zara's words. Of course she would. They had been best friends since high school.

Humans and shifters had lived alongside each other for decades now. Zara knew everything about her, and Marley knew all there was about her. She'd sat by Zara's side through countless broken relationships and life events. She'd do anything to help Zara because of her one secret that she'd harbored since the day they'd met.

Zara was her mate.

She'd been in love with her best bud since she was sixteen years old. Fourteen years later, and Marley still refused to let her know. It crushed Marley's heart little by little to watch Zara be with the men in her past. She never wanted to risk losing Zara so instead of pouring out her heart, she'd decided to be friends with her. She'd rather have Zara in her life as a companion than to not have her at all.

A smile lingered on her lips as she imagined her friend. She was sure that Zara was sprawled out on her couch, with her blonde hair in a perfect messy bun, a pair of tiny shorts on and a cami.

Her wolf rumbled in her chest slightly with the vision coming to mind. Zara had the perfect curves that Marley ached to be able to discover. Her full breasts drove Marley crazy. The tiny tanks she wore around her apartment displayed them perfectly. Of course, as best friends over the years, they'd seen each other naked. Her mouth watered just imagining being able to pull Zara's small cami down to reveal her dusky-pink areolae.

She grew slick with need while she lay in her bed listening to her mate speak of her plans for the trip and the final things she needed to do before they left.

Zara's husky voice put Marley on edge. She slowly trailed her fingers down her neck to her naked breasts. Marley hated sleeping in clothes. It was the shifter in her. If she didn't have to wear them, she wouldn't. The nude body didn't bother shifters. Clothes never survived a quick shift, and when she reverted back to her human form, she would be naked.

She pushed the thin blanket off her, leaving her body exposed. Her nipples beaded from the touch of the cool air in her bedroom. She bit her lip, stopping to tug on her tight buds, imagining Zara was nipping them with her teeth.

"How many bathing suits are you packing?" Zara asked.

"About three or four," she replied, managing to not sound breathless. She didn't want to give away her current actions. She'd masturbated countless times to the fantasy of Zara.

"Okay, good. Then I don't feel bad packing five." Zara chuckled. "I'm bringing the one I picked up when we went shopping last week."

Marley bit back a groan thinking of the suit that Zara mentioned. It was a tiny bikini that showed off everything but her areolae and mons. She continued with her hand exploration and quickly made it to her soaked labia.

"It was cute," she murmured, listening to Zara rattle on.

She let loose a silent gasp when she parted her folds and found her pussy to be drenched. There wasn't a day that she didn't walk around Zara painfully aroused. It might be best that her friend was human and couldn't scent her arousal when they were together.

Marley took a deep breath and slowly slid her fingers along her swollen nub. Her clit ached to feel Zara's lips around it. Biting back a groan as she dove her fingers deep into her core. She dropped her legs open to give her full access to herself. She pulled out of her pussy and trailed her arousal up to her clit and massaged, applying pressure on it. Her release was already close to the surface.

"Marley?"

"Yeah?" she answered, trying to control her breath.

"Are you going to sleep on me?" Zara asked.

She wished, but then again, if she got the chance to be in the bed with Zara, there wouldn't be any sleeping.

"No." She closed her eyes tight, fighting back the moans that wanted to pour from her mouth. Her fingers were frantically flicking her clitoris. She was desperate for her pending release.

"Yes, you are. We'll finish talking tomorrow."

"I'm up." She chuckled but guessed Zara wasn't trying to hear her.

"Nope, I'll see you tomorrow. Goodnight."

The sound of the call disconnecting filled Marley's ears. She lived alone in a small home on pack grounds and didn't have to be as quiet.

"Oh God," she groaned, reaching over to her nightstand. She pulled out her handy-dandy vibrator and flipped the ON switch. Her body was strung tight, and she need this release. Marley had been in a state of sexual frustration since the minute Zara had called her. The sound of its purr was music to her ears. She lined it up to her soaked opening and plunged it home.

The clit stimulator brushed against her sensitive

bundle of nerves with each thrust. Her back arched off the bed as her orgasm slammed into her.

"Zara!" she cried out while the waves of the hard climax rolled over her. She thrust the vibrator in and out of her pulsating core, wishing Zara was there with her. She slowly came down from her euphoric journey and knew it wouldn't happen.

Zara wasn't into females. Over the years, she'd only dated males. Marley's body grew still as she tried to control her breathing with that thought. She'd come to the realization that she'd always been the friend a long time ago.

She pulled her toy from her slick core and turned it off. She glanced down at it and laughed, seeing it glistening with an abundance of her juices. She brought it to her lips and cleaned it off with her tongue.

If only Zara realized how much she loved her, maybe that could all change.

CHAPTER TWO

Zara hung up with a smile. She could always tell when Marley was about to doze off. Her friend's breathing had changed on the phone, signaling that she was falling fast asleep even though she'd tried to admit she wasn't.

Zara knew Marley better than she knew herself. They had been longtime pals, meeting at the young age of sixteen. They'd become fast friends and had been inseparable. Zara never once cared that Marley was a shifter. She actually loved Marley's wolf. She was a pretty black beast whose eyes displayed Marley's personality.

A yawn escaped her as she stretched on her couch. Her t-shirt rode up on her stomach. The cold air on her belly sent a chill down her spine.

"Okay, I guess it's time for me to go to bed, too," she mumbled, standing from her couch. She turned off all the lights and television before making her way to her bedroom. Her small apartment was just the right size for her. She had a second bedroom but had converted it into an office. She was a full-time author and needed a designated space to be able to write her masterpieces.

Excitement filled her with the thought of the upcoming trip. Sun, ocean, and writing. It was the perfect combination to help her get over Bo. Her ass of an ex-boyfriend had cheated on her. She'd been so caught up in her work that she hadn't seen the signs until it was too late.

She flicked the light on once she passed through the door and cringed. She'd totally forgotten that she'd left all of the clothes she planned to pack up for the trip spread out on her bed.

"No time like the present to actually pack." She pushed a few of her wayward strands of hair out of her face while she walked over to her closet to search for her suitcase.

This trip would be good for her. She needed a break from the world. Thankfully, her and Bo had never moved in together like he had started hinting at. Something in her gut had kept her from giving in to him. She'd always been independent and wanted to keep her own place. He'd just pouted and acted like he was upset, but she knew how to distract him from the conversations. She'd kneel in front of him and suck his cock, leaving him to 'forgive' her and not bring it up for a while.

She bit her lip, placing the suitcase on her bed. She and Bo had been good together. They'd played games like that all the time. Sexual games were a fun way for them to release pent-up tension or make up for when they were upset at each other. She had thought that there could have been a future for them, but it would seem there wouldn't be.

There would be no coming back from him cheating on her.

No more thinking about Bo, she commanded herself.

A deep sigh escaped her as she folded her clothes. Marley had warned her about packing heavy. Lucky enough, since they would be on the ocean with the plans to stop at few places, her swim suits would probably be worn the most.

"Me and my bestie sailing the ocean." She laughed.

Marley was the best thing in her life. She had been with her through thick and thin. Zara didn't know where she'd be without Marley.

Her bestie was tall, beautiful, and a wolf shifter. Maybe it was the beast in her that made her so protective of Zara. She knew that she never had to doubt Marley's loyalty. Zara wished that her friend would find her mate. She was slightly jealous that shifters had something ingrained in their brain to signal who was the perfect match for them. Humans were left to figure it out on their own, most getting it wrong.

Marley had the patience of a saint. Zara, on the other hand, was dying to find the one for her. She was ready to settle down and start a family. She was thirty, and her biological clock was ticking.

It was no surprise that Marley had suggested the trip. She was from a powerful shifter family who owned a large boating company. She had been joking with Marley when she'd asked about her wolf and the water. Over the years, she had grown to know much about wolves and knew they were great swimmers—their shifter counterparts were no different.

"Finally," she groaned, closing her suitcase. She dragged it over against the wall across from her bed, knowing she would have to make sure she packed everything she would need.

She climbed into the bed and grabbed her laptop that sat charging on her nightstand. She was naturally a night owl and did a lot of her writing in the bed. It was something about the quietness in the air once the town settled that helped her creative juices flow.

After logging on to her computer, she began going through her emails. There were perks to being a full-time author. She could do her job anywhere in the world. Three weeks on the open waters was a writer's dream. She envisioned lying out on the sundeck with her laptop and smiled. Marley's idea was perfect, and Zara couldn't wait to leave. They would be flying over to Hawaii, and then the two of them would be off on their adventure.

"Are you sure the girls will be safe?" Jena Gerwulf asked with a worried look plastered on her face.

Marley glanced at her mother and recognized how much they mirrored each other. Her mother didn't appear a day over forty, but it was the shifter genes. Wolves were slow to age, and Jena Gerwulf was pushing sixty-five years old. Both of Marley's parents seemed younger than their appearance. They were at their prime.

They all stood by the private jet that would fly them to Hawaii. Her family was a close-knit group and had accepted Zara.

"They will be fine," Evan Gerwulf grumbled. His lips spread into a wide smile while he held his arms open.

Marley laughed at her mother's pained expression. She leaned into her father as he collapsed his arms around her.

"You girls be extra careful," her mother urged, tugging Zara into a hug.

"Yes, Mrs. Gerwulf." Zara's voice was muffled against Jena's chest.

"Your mother's right. Be careful. I know you know the yacht like the back of your hand. Plot your course—"

"Dad, I know. You've taught me well." Marley laughed, pulling back from her father's embrace. Her eyes met Zara's, and they shared a giggle as they stepped away from Marley's parents. "I'll call you before we leave Hawaii, okay? I promise."

Her father nodded. "That will be good."

She walked over and grabbed her mother, squeezing her tight.

"I love you, Mom," she whispered in her ear.

Her mother returned her fierce hug.

"I love you, too. Make sure you pay attention to the weather," her mother advised, leaning back. She gripped Marley's face and placed a loving kiss on her cheek.

"Yes, ma'am." She smiled and waved to both of them. "Let's go, bestie."

They turned and made their way onto the private plane. The crew introduced themselves and helped them settle in their plush leather recliners.

"It's ridiculous how much money your family has," Zara remarked, snapping her safety belt in place. She had the window seat and pressed her face up against the glass.

"Why? It's generational money. Passed down from my great-great—I forgot how many greats—grandfathers down to my father." She settled back in her seat and watched the crew while they closed the hatch to the plane and prepared for takeoff. She glanced over at Zara and almost forgot to breathe.

Her thick blonde hair was braided and rested on

her shoulder. Her summer dress stopped at the knee, sending Marley's wolf pacing. Everything about her friend was feminine and soft. Marley swallowed hard when her gaze trailed down to Zara's shoulders, not seeing any signs of a bra.

Shit.

"I'm just saying, some of us poor, starving authors—"

"Oh, puh-lease." Marley rolled her eyes at her friend's overdramatization. Yes, her family was worth a few billion, but Zara was far from starving. She was a very popular writer with a crazy following that snatched up every book she released. She was doing quite well for herself and wasn't hurting for anything.

"Would you ladies like champagne?" the stewardess, Amelia, asked, standing next to them with a bottle and two flutes.

Marley glanced at Zara, and they burst out in a fit of laughter. Okay, maybe her family did have way too much money, but they were about to take a trip of a lifetime.

"Why the hell not," Zara quipped, wiping the tears from her face.

Amelia smiled and poured the bubbly liquid into

their glasses. They turned to each other once she walked away.

"To an amazing trip with my bestie," Zara said, holding her glass up.

"May we have the time of our lives."

CHAPTER THREE

"This boat is amazing," Zara exclaimed, eyeing the living quarters. It was a small area that housed a living room, dining room, and kitchen all in one. In one corner, there was a pilot's chair and steering wheel with a navigational computer.

This was one of the smaller yachts that the Gerwulfs owned. She'd been on their larger ones that could sleep twenty people. But this one was cozy. According to Marley, it was meant for four to five people.

But it would just be the two of them.

She breathed in a sigh, seeing where she could sit her laptop. The makeshift dining table was just big enough for her computer to be set up. The yacht came equipped with Wi-Fi, which would help Zara with some of her work. She couldn't wait to share pictures with her readers. She planned to take amazing photos while they were on the ocean to share in her weekly newsletter she sent out.

"This is one of the smaller ones, but we didn't need bigger," Marley replied, coming down the stairs. Her keen blue eyes seemed to take everything in at once.

Zara took a deep breath and tried to beat down the nervous butterflies that fluttered in her stomach.

She took in Marley's perfectly tanned skin that was displayed by her dress that covered her bathing suit. She'd never been one to have a problem complimenting a beautiful woman, but at the moment she didn't know why she felt nervous.

She'd been on many trips with Marley before, but it was something about the predatory gleam in Marley's eye that took her breath away. Zara shook her head with a laugh.

I need sun and fresh air, she thought to herself.

"Looks like we have everything we need." The cabinets were fully stocked with nonperishables.

"A good sailor is always prepared." Marley smirked, leaning against the counter. "We have enough food to last six months if need be."

"But we are only going on a three-week expedition." Zara cocked her head to the side.

"Yes, but we have to play it safe. Whatever we don't use will remain in the boat. This is one of the yachts we rent out to private customers who want to sail."

"Oh, okay," Zara breathed. It was scary to think something could happen to the boat, but she pushed that thought aside. Marley knew what she was doing, and they would be safe.

Marley was in her element. Zara trusted her friend knew what she was talking about.

"Let me give you a tour and a safety rundown of where everything is. We are set to leave before first light in the morning."

"Aye-aye, Captain." Zara giggled, playfully saluting Marley.

"Move your arse." Marley's bad imitation of a pirate made them laugh even harder as they walked up the stairs to the main deck.

Zara was met with the sight of the stunning Hawaiian skyline. The sun was setting, but the day was still warm and beautiful. She trailed behind Marley as she gave her an official tour of the upper cockpit and explained how this particular vessel had two places it could be navigated.

"This is a fine-looking boat." She sighed, following Marley.

"Thanks. If we need them, here is where the distress flares and fire extinguishers are kept." Marley pointed to a cabinet.

"Wow, this is a little intense," she murmured, rubbing her arms. She'd been cruising with Marley and her family before, but never anything this long. Usually a weekend of fun and then they'd dock, but this was an eye-opener for her.

"Lifeboat is this way." Marley motioned for Zara to follow her.

They walked toward the back of the yacht and took the stairs that led them to the swim deck.

They stood on the deck and gazed out onto the ocean. Zara became lost in the beauty of the Hawaiian skies and air.

"I really appreciate this." She sighed, turning to Marley whose eyes softened.

"I know. We are going to return and come back brand-new women, especially you." Marley opened her arms and motioned to Zara for a hug.

With a great laugh, she stepped forward and wrapped her arms around her.

"You are the best friend a girl could have," she murmured, squeezing her tight before stepping away.

Her heart skipped a beat at the intensity of Marley's eyes.

It has to be her animal. Maybe she needs to shift.

"Let's get our girls' trip started right. I believe there is a very large bottle of wine with our name on it," Marley suggested with a wide grin. The strange look in her eyes was no longer present.

"Yeah, wine sounds good right about now." Zara nodded, her gaze following Marley's figure up the stairs. Zara's feet were frozen in place as she watched Marley's hips sway back and forth. Marley paused and turned back to look at Zara who quickly averted her eyes.

"You coming?"

"Yes, was just admiring the view," she lied, waving toward the lowering sun. Her feet carried her to the stairs. She swallowed hard, unsure of what was going on. Maybe the fresh air was having the opposite effect on her than what she needed. If she didn't know any better, she had actually admired Marley's ass.

Was she attracted to her best friend?

"Welp, that bottle is gone." Marley giggled, tossing

their empty wine jug in the trash can. She needed something to help relax her, and sharing the best merlot always did the trick. They had both slipped into their jammies and lounged around on the couch in the main galley to enjoy each others company and a very large bottle of wine. She had a slight buzz—nothing that would prevent her from getting up before dawn for them to depart.

"Oh my. That was so good. I say we open another one," Zara offered before tipping her head back to finish off the last of her drink.

"Nope. We have sail at first light, and I can't navigate tipsy," Marley scoffed. It would take a lot for her to get drunk. Shifters' metabolism burned through alcohol extremely fast. That would be the last thing she'd need—getting a ticket for skippering a boat under the influence.

They had plenty of time for getting drunk once they were on the open ocean. A fun little fact about this model yacht was it had an autopilot option which could come in handy later.

"You're being a party pooper." Zara pouted, crossing her arms in front of her chest.

Marley laughed, trying to keep her eyes off Zara's mounds that were pushed up by her arms. Her wolf scratched at her abdomen with a whimper.

"Down girl," she muttered.

She had been fighting her wolf all evening. Her animal was demanding to come forward. She had shifted and gone for a run yesterday to allow her beast to stretch its legs. There would be no telling when she'd get to shift again.

"Come on. Time for bed." She was cut off by Zara's fake whine. "Let's go."

Marley stood and grabbed her tipsy friend's arm, pulling her to her feet. Zara stumbled slightly and leaned into Marley. They both laughed while Marley guided Zara toward her cabin.

They had played a silly game of rock, paper, scissors in order to claim the master bedroom when they'd arrived, with Zara winning.

"Hmmm...you smell good," Zara mumbled, turning her nose to Marley. She inhaled deeply and released her breath.

The heated air blew across Marley's arm and sent a shiver along her spine.

Marley bit her lip and held back a groan. This was their first night, and they had three more weeks together.

"Thank you, my dear," she exhaled. Her nipples pushed painfully against her tank, and she willed them down. "Here we go." She guided Zara into the cabin. Her eyes adjusted to the darkness, allowing her to maneuver her tipsy friend to the bed.

"Oh, this mattress is so comfy." Zara groaned after flopping into the bed.

Marley tried to keep her eyes off Zara's smooth, tan legs while reaching for the blanket. She quickly pulled it up and covered the tempting flesh of the woman she desired.

"Sweet dreams, bestie," Marley murmured. Her gaze lingered on Zara's soft lips that parted and released a soft snore. She watched, fascinated, as Zara's tongue slipped out and moistened her lips. She bit her own to keep from leaning in and taking a taste.

She hastily made her way from the room and entered her own cabin before letting out a deep breath.

That was a close call.

She ached to climb in the bed with Zara. What she wouldn't give to be able to hold Zara close in her arms. She disrobed and folded her clothes before placing them on the shelving unit beside her bed. There was no way she could sleep with clothes on, even on the boat.

The slight buzz she had was wearing off. She climbed into her bed, her body relaxing. They'd had a long day of travel. The flight to Hawaii had been lengthy, and they'd barely stopped once they'd landed on the big island. They had driven straight to the pier and boarded the boat.

"Marley!" Zara's drunken voice called out from her cabin.

Marley's shifter ears picked up movement in the other room. "Yes?"

"I love you, bestie!"

Marley smiled as she snuggled down beneath her blanket. "I love you, too, Zara."

CHAPTER FOUR

Music blasted through the speakers that were placed around the boat, and Zara danced around her small cabin. It was designed to sleep two people, and Zara could not see a couple sharing the area. It was a tight fit with just her in the room. They would not be to walk past each other while in the compact space.

Singing along with the music, she opened her drawer and had a hard time deciding which bathing suit to wear.

"What the hell," she muttered, grabbed the black two-piece, and shut the drawer. She shook her bottom to the beat and proceeded to slide the suit on. Glancing in the mirror, she put her hair up in a messy bun, wanting to get some sun and didn't want her hair in the way.

"Love in an elevator," she sang along with the song. "Livin' it up when I'm going down. Love in an elevator."

She twirled around and realized she'd tied the straps of her bikini top and couldn't get the back part done up. She grabbed her sunglasses before opening the door and went in search of Marley, still singing along with one of the best bands of all time.

Not seeing her friend in the main galley, she headed to the upper deck in search of the boat's captain. She'd woken this morning to the gentle sway of the boat rocking. She had opened her eyes, finding the sun shining into her cabin. Zara had known Marley wanted to leave at the crack of dawn, but she'd thought she would have woken her up.

"Ahoy there," Marley called out as Zara stepped onto the deck.

Her eyes adjusted to the bright sun. Even with the awning to provide shade over the captain's chair, the glare from the sun was still unforgiving.

"Morning." Zara smiled, walking over to Marley.

Her friend looked comfortable behind the wheel. Her flawless tanned skin was accented by her blue bikini which matched the color of her eyes.

"Would you mind?" Zara presented her back for Marley.

"Did you sleep well?"

Marley tugged on the suit before taking the ties and knotting them behind her.

"I did. Why didn't you wake me when you got up?" she asked, turning to face Marley who shrugged a shoulder.

"You were snoring too good. I didn't have the heart to wake you. Besides, we've only been sailing for two hours."

"But I could have kept—"

"You needed the sleep. Those tiny bags beneath your eyes are almost gone already."

"Hey!" Zara chuckled, reaching up with her fingertips to smooth out her face. "It's not been that bad."

"Did you have breakfast?" Marley asked.

"No, not yet. I'm going to head down and make me a small bite. Want anything?"

"No, I'm good. I had some fruit. You might want to eat some. I bought it for us to have for the first few days, otherwise, it will just go bad."

"Sounds good." Zara patted Marley on the back and turned to go down below. "I'll return soon. Holler if you need me," she shouted over her shoulder. In the kitchen, she snatched some fruit and yogurt out of the refrigerator. She cut up her apple and threw some grapes in a bowl.

She sat at the makeshift dining table and booted up her laptop. She'd check her emails and sales while she ate. Afterwards, she was going to spend the first day of her vacation actually relaxing. Maybe later she'd write.

It took her longer than expected since she had a few emails where the responses needed were more detail-oriented. She finished off the yogurt and cruised through her sales reports. Pleased everything looked to be doing well, she snapped the laptop shut and smiled.

"Vacation time." She stood and walked into her cabin to grab her sunscreen, a towel, her cell, and earphones. It was time to go sunbathing.

Her feet carried her to the upper deck, and she strolled over to the sundeck.

"I thought you had got lost down there." Marley chuckled.

"Nope. Had to take care of some business first, but now I'm officially on vacation." She laughed. She gripped her camera and took a few pictures of the Pacific and even a selfie. "Time to work on this tan of mine."

"I'm coming. Let me just put the boat on autopilot." Marley ambled out onto the sundeck and joined her. She laid out her towel next to Zara's and flopped down. Her face was partially covered by her ostentatiously large sunglasses.

Zara squirted some of the sunscreen into her hands and lathered her legs and arms up. She didn't want to risk the chance of being burned while on holiday. It would be the most horrible thing that could happen and ruin a vacation if she had to walk around with painful skin.

"So how long until we make land in Tahiti?" she asked, rubbing the cream into her skin.

Marley grabbed the bottle and proceeded to follow suit.

"It should take us about four to six days. It depends on the weather."

They had planned to dock the boat and stay in Tahiti for about a week before slowly making their way back. Zara imagined once docked and lounging on the sandy beaches, she would get some great writing in.

"Can you get my back, please?" she asked, holding up the tube.

"Um, sure." Marley grabbed it from her hands while she flipped over onto her stomach. "Do you want me to untie you to keep you from having tan lines?"

"Sure. I guess there is no one for miles around. Topless tanning it is then." Zara laughed, feeling a tug on the ties on her suit. She pulled it off and placed it on the deck near her head, decision made. It was just her and Marley, and they'd certainly seen each other naked over the years.

"When in Rome," Marley murmured, flinging her top on the deck.

Zara's gaze flickered to her friend's full breasts, and she swallowed. They were beautiful. She quickly turned away and laid flat on her stomach while Marley scooted over to her.

She closed her eyes with the first touch of Marley's hands on her back. She slowly rubbed the cream into Zara's skin, massaging as she went.

Zara bit her lip to keep from moaning aloud. Marley's hands were magic, sliding down the curve of her back. Her magical fingertips worked Zara's muscles. Her nipples grew sensitive, pressing into the towel beneath her. With each stroke of Marley's hands on her flesh, Zara realized she was growing aroused.

What in the hell?

She'd never had this reaction to her friend

before. They'd put sunscreen on each other at least a hundred times over the years.

But now it was as if her body was trying to tell her something.

Marley's firm hands drifted lower to the curve of her back, and this time a moan escaped from Zara's lips.

"Enjoying it?" Marley's husky voice sounded, breaking into her thoughts.

A low growl echoed in the air, and Zara's core clenched.

Marley's wolf was near.

Zara had heard the rumble plenty of times and was taught shifters sometimes had to battle their animals to stay in their human form. She swallowed hard, her ears picking up the sound again.

"Yes," she breathed, trying to get control of herself. Her mind was racing, attempting to understand what was going on. Her pussy was slick with need. She bit her lip and internally shook her head.

This was Marley.

Her best friend.

"When did you get training as a masseuse?" Zara forced a chuckle in an attempt to break this spell over her.

"I like a good massage here and there. I just do

what the masseuses do to me." She laughed, pulling away from Zara.

Zara sat up on her elbows and eyed Marley lying on her back.

"Need me to do you?" she asked.

"Nah, I'm good. Shifters don't burn, and if I did, my skin would just heal."

"I'm totally jealous," she muttered, laying her head down on her folded arms. Behind her sunglasses, she took the time to study Marley, truly seeing her for the first time. Marley was a beautiful, sensual woman. Being a shifter, she was more in tune with her sexual nature. Her dark hair was arranged in a bun, with wisps escaping. Her perfect, full breasts sat on her chest with tightly budded nipples.

Zara's breaths deepened.

She couldn't look away from the full mounds. Secretly, she wondered what it would feel like to rub hers against Marley's. Curiosity was getting the better of her. What was it like to suckle another woman's breasts? Would hard nipples be soft to her tongue's touch? She'd only ever had the pleasure of rubbing her own clit and slipping her fingers in her own core. What would it feel like to slide her finger between another woman's slick labia?

Her mind was riddled with questions that only intensified her arousal.

This is my best friend, she muttered to herself internally. *Get a grip.*

She turned her head away to keep her gaze from roaming Marley's body again. She willed herself to cool down, but she was painfully aroused. With her eyes closed, she tried to work on the plot of her book in her head and erase her erotic thoughts of her best friend from her mind.

With Marley lying beside her, that was going to be hard to do.

CHAPTER FIVE

Marley narrowed her eyes on the storm clouds rolling in. Their second day had started off with a beautiful clear sky. They'd just had lunch a couple of hours ago on the sundeck, and Zara had disappeared below to write. But now, angry dark clouds were rushing toward the boat. She glanced down at the navigation screen before her in an attempt to replot their course.

This was going to be one hell of a storm.

She'd sailed in severe weather in the past and knew they could ride it out, but her wolf was pacing.

It didn't like the look of the sky either.

Something was off.

The winds picked up, whipping her hair around

her face. She pushed the offending strands away as she went into survivor mode.

She was sort of glad to have a distraction to keep her mind from yesterday's tanning session on the sundeck. The feel of Zara's soft skin underneath her fingers was a form of torture she'd be willing to undergo anytime. Her nose had picked up Zara's arousal, and it had taken everything she had to not flip her over and have her way with her.

Her attention was snapped back to the computer screen. Alarms blared with a warning.

Fat drops of rain poured on the deck. She rushed and grabbed the emergency flare and life vests, just in case.

"Is everything okay?" Zara asked, coming up the stairs.

"Storm. Let's ride it out below," Marley suggested. She didn't want to give away that she was nervous.

Zara's eyes widened at the sight of the jackets.

"Just a precaution." Marley passed the vests to Zara who collapsed them against her chest and disappeared below.

The ocean was not to be taken for granted. It could be a beast. She didn't fear it so much, but she had a lot of respect for nature.

Marley jogged down the stairs and turned, closing the door that led to above.

The wailing sounds of wind filled the cabin. Their yacht was a solidly made boat and should be able to withstand the force of the water.

Her heart raced as she sat in the captain's chair in front of the second navigator computer.

"Should we send out a distress signal?"

Marley shook her head. "Not yet. Let's see what this does. I wouldn't want to call for help if it blows over quickly. The clouds were rolling pretty fast. Ocean storms can be fickle."

The wind died down, but the sounds of the patter of rain echoed around them. The boat continued to rock with the waves while the storm increased.

"It came quick. I was just working on my book, and before I knew it, my laptop kept trying to slide away from me." Zara gave a nervous chuckle.

"It literally appeared out of nowhere." Marley shook her head. Nature was a wonder. One could never truly predict what the elements would do, especially out on the open waters.

"We're going to be okay, right?"

Marley picked up on the scent of Zara's fear,

leaving her animal to pace inside her chest. She turned to face Zara and nodded.

"Just hang on. Write or something to keep your mind distracted. We'll be fine." She would never let anything happen to Zara. Her wolf would protect Zara with her last dying breath if need be.

"You promise?" Zara's wide eyes met hers.

Go to her, her wolf growled.

Marley stood from her seat and walked over to Zara. She knelt in front of her and reached out a hand. She slid her fingers along her cheek. Her heart skipped a beat as Zara leaned into her touch.

"Have I ever let you down?" Her voice grew thick with emotion. There was not a day that had gone by in the years since they'd met where Marley wasn't supporting Zara or protecting her.

The boat rocked hard, almost sending them both tumbling to the floor. Zara gripped her hand and shook her head.

"Never," she whispered, blatant trust brimming in her gem-green eyes.

"Secure everything, and let's ride this out." She pushed off the floor and stalked back over to the wheel, taking it off the autopilot and focusing on controlling the boat.

Zara moved around the area as she worked to put up things they had left lying out.

The howling of the wind picked up, as did the rocking of the boat. The sounds were deafening.

The storm has officially arrived.

Zara's scream cut through the air, followed by a thump with the boat tipping to the side.

"Hang on!" Marley shouted, trying to turn the wheel. She looked out the window and was unable to see through the darkness.

This wasn't good.

The lights in the cabin went out, basking them in the cover of blackness.

Marley released a curse, using her strength to get the wheel to turn the opposite way. Teachings from her father echoed in her head as she tried her best to skipper the boat.

The computers went out.

"Shit," she muttered, trying to keep her voice down where Zara couldn't hear her. Without the computers, she wouldn't be able to see where on earth they were.

If the computers and electricity didn't turn back on, she'd have to use her backup.

An old-fashioned compass and maps.

She sent up a prayer this storm would quickly blow over.

"Are you okay, Zara?" she called out.

"Yeah. I just got tossed on the floor, but I'm good," Zara shouted.

Marley's wolf settled down a little but was on edge. The ocean was being unforgiving. She didn't know who'd pissed the bitch off, Mother Nature, but she was taking the brunt of her anger out on their yacht.

A large crashing sounded above. An electric current zipped through the air, and the hairs on Marley's arms rose. The scent of something burning met her.

Marley knew her wolf's nose had picked up the faint smell well before Zara would.

She bit back a curse.

The boat had been struck by lightning.

Zara had never been so scared in her life before. The storm finally settled down. Marley seemed to think they were in the eye of it and went up to take a look at the damage. Worry filled her as the smell of something burning met her nose once Marley disappeared up the stairs.

Just thinking how they were in the middle of the ocean and basically trapped if the boat couldn't start again.

This would make a great plot to a book. She laughed at the thought.

The day had been perfect. She'd gotten quite a few words down on her latest romantic suspense. Her body had been riddled with anxiety from her carnal thoughts she'd had the day before about Marley. She still didn't know what to think about them.

Since then, she'd had a hard time keeping her eyes off Marley so she'd buried her face in her laptop and pounded away on the keyboard.

Her attention was drawn to Marley returning. Her face was grim, sending Zara's heart racing.

Something was wrong.

"What's the matter?" she asked, watching Marley close the door again, shutting them off from the elements.

"Lightning hit the boat, killing the computers."

"You can navigate the boat without them, right?" Nervous, she brushed a hand through her hair. They'd still be okay. She knew Marley had been trained well by her father in the art of sailing, and this should be a no-brainer.

Her gaze followed Marley who paced the small area. Zara could clearly see the wolf in Marley. The way she walked through the tiny space was that of a brooding wolf. Her movements didn't help Zara's anxiety.

The computers weren't the only issue.

"The engine is shot. I can't get it to start, and with it being dark, I can't try to do anything until morning where I have more light."

Marley stopped her pacing and faced Zara. Her shoulders slumped slightly, and Zara got up from the couch. She padded over to her friend and stood before her.

"It will be okay. We'll float tonight, and in the morning you can check it out. We'll be fine," she breathed. She didn't know where she was getting the confidence, but her gut told her everything would work itself out. She reach out and drew Marley into a tight hug. Her breath caught in her throat at the feel of Marley pressed against her. Their thin bathing suits were the only things separating them.

Marley returned the hug with a tight squeeze. She was taller than Zara and rested her chin on the top of Zara's head. She tucked her face in the nape of Marley's neck and held on.

"There's no one else I'd rather be stuck in the middle of nowhere with." Marley chuckled, pulling back. Her crisp blue eyes smiled down at her.

"And I you." Zara winked at her, and they both giggled, breaking up the tension.

"Thanks, I needed that."

"What are best friends for? You planned this entire trip for me, and it's the least I can do. Comfort you during an emergency."

They stared at each other before bursting out in good, hearty laughter.

"Well, let's get settled for tonight. In the morning we'll try to fix the engine," Marley said. "I think the brunt of the storm has passed, but there are more clouds coming this way. It's going to be a long night."

CHAPTER SIX

The constant howl of the wind filled the air. The boat rocked with every wave crashing up against it. After her assessment of the yacht, Marley determined it had held up well aside from the engine and all the electricity. She'd have to put on her mechanic's cap and see if she could get it to work tomorrow.

She shifted in her bed and pulled the covers up. The cabins were a little cooler with the weather. Once the final leg of the storm passed, it should warm up by morning.

Her ears perked up, hearing movement from Zara's cabin, and seconds later, Zara's form appeared in her doorway.

"Everything all right?" Marley asked, propping

up on one elbow. Her eyes had adjusted in the dark, but it was because of her wolf. She was sure for Zara it was completely dark.

"Do you mind if I sleep in here with you? I swear I'm still a little freaked out," Zara admitted. "And it's freezing in my room."

Marley swallowed hard, knowing she was completely naked beneath the covers.

The gods were playing a dirty game with her.

"Um, sure. Come in," she replied.

Zara didn't waste any time diving in the bed and sliding beneath the covers. Due to the cabin's small size, the bed was compact, and there was no way they could sleep without bumping into each other.

"Oh my goodness. You are a furnace." Zara's teeth chattering could be heard. She scooted over and brought her body flush with Marley.

The scent of Zara drove her animal wild. Her gums ached and burned as her canines tried to descend. She fought the wolf inside her and forced her fangs to remain hidden.

The sound of Zara's gasp filled the air as she came to the realization Marley was naked.

"Here, let me put something on," she uttered, not wanting to offend Zara.

"No, you're fine. It's not like I haven't seen you

naked before. I'm freezing, and the heat is pouring off you. Don't you dare move." She tucked herself into Marley's side, snuggling into the crook of her arm. Her warm breath blew across Marley's collarbone.

"Okay," she murmured. Her body was strung tight. The feel of Zara lying in her arms was heaven. She turned and pulled Zara fully into her embrace.

The rocking of the boat became soothing and settled her animal slightly. Her beast was pleased Zara had come to them when she was afraid and was loving every minute of her being in their arms. She breathed in deep and inhaled Zara's unique scent. She paused, catching the hint of arousal coming from Zara.

Marley swallowed hard.

The need for this woman she was holding burned something fierce in her chest.

It was now or never.

She glanced down at Zara and brushed her hair away from her face. She tenderly trailed her fingers down the side of Zara's cheek. Zara's quick intake of breath reached Marley's ears. Even in the dark, her shifter vision allowed her to see Zara's gaze was on her.

She lowered her face to Zara's and covered her

mouth with hers. Her heart raced as Zara's soft lips parted, granting her tongue entrance. Their lips moved over each other in the softest of kisses. Marley swept her tongue into Zara's mouth, coaxing hers to come duel and play with hers.

Zara's hand slid along her shoulder and up to the nape of her neck, anchoring Marley to her.

She could have wept with relief at the sigh of acceptance. The kiss deepened before turning urgent. She shifted their bodies where she could lean over Zara who immediately opened her legs to allow Marley to settle into the valley of her thighs.

She pulled her head back and gazed into Zara's eyes. They were both breathing fast.

"Zara, are you sure?" she whispered.

"Kiss me, Marley." Zara tugged her face back to hers.

Their lips fused into a hot, open, wet kiss. Marley slid her hands along Zara's body and discovered she only had a small cami and panties on.

With Marley's excitement, her hands partially shifted, and she ripped the side of Zara's shirt and underwear. She tore her lips from Zara and pulled the offending items off, tossing them over her shoulder. She leaned back on her knees and took in the shadow of Zara's naked body lying on the bed.

"Hold on. I want to see you," Marley uttered. She reached over to the nightstand and clicked on her battery-powered lamp. It was for emergency use only so they could reserve the batteries, and this was a definite emergency. The soft light filled the cabin, revealing Zara's dusky-rose areolae, soft abdomen, and hairless mons.

She licked her lips as the smell of Zara's arousal grew stronger.

"I like it when you look at me like that," Zara admitted softly. "I've seen it so many times. I always thought it was your animal, but now I know. How did I not see the truth?"

"Shh... Don't worry. We can talk about it later," Marley promised. Right now, she wanted to discover Zara's body properly. She'd waited so long for this day, and now it was here, she was going to take her time.

She placed a kiss on Zara's mouth before trailing her lips and tongue down her chin and neck. She headed straight for Zara's soft mounds.

The memory of their topless tanning came to mind. A growl vibrated in her chest at the thought of how Zara's breasts had swayed with her every movement when she had flipped onto her back the day before.

She enclosed her lips around Zara's taut nipple, and Zara let loose a gasp. Marley sucked as much of the breast into her mouth as possible. She wanted to taste with every part of Zara as she could.

Zara's fingers threaded themselves in her hair and held her to her chest as Marley used the flat of her tongue to bathe both breasts. She paid closed attention to them, and Zara writhed beneath her.

"Marley," Zara whispered, her hips thrusting against Marley's abdomen.

Marley was on a mission. She trailed her tongue along Zara's belly. She dipped her tongue into Zara's navel, taking a second to breath in, loving the strong scent of Zara's arousal.

Marley's core clenched with the knowledge Zara was this aroused because of her. She was anxious to have the taste of Zara on her tongue, therefore, she continued her exploration. She moved and brought her eyes level with Zara's smooth, pink labia. She licked her lips as Zara spread her legs wide.

Marley took notice of the moisture seeping from Zara's pussy.

"You are beautiful," Marley murmured, using a finger to trace along Zara's slit.

"Please," Zara urged, her body trembling.

"Do you want me to taste you, Zara?" She

dipped her finger into Zara's warm core, sliding in effortlessly thanks to her honey. She pulled her finger out and licked it, her eyes rolling at the first taste of Zara. It was a taste she could only describe as Zara.

"Yes. Please, Marley. Make me come," Zara begged.

"As you wish." She spread Zara's labia, revealing her swollen clitoris. With the flat pad of her tongue, she took one long swipe of Zara's pussy.

Zara released a shout, her back arching from the bed. The full taste of her sweet goodness exploded on Marley's tongue. With a growl, she feasted on Zara's slick pussy. She used her tongue to draw Zara's juices toward her clit. She suckled it, loving how Zara's fingers tightened in her hair.

Marley cupped Zara's ass to bring her to her mouth. She wasn't afraid to consume all of Zara. She'd waited what seemed a lifetime to be able to do this and she'd make sure Zara couldn't think of no one but her.

She trailed her tongue down to Zara's puckered hole and promised herself she would explore it later. She moved back up and latched on to Zara's swollen nub. She hummed and shook her head.

"Oh God!" Zara called out, thrusting her pussy

farther into Marley's mouth.

Marley inserted two fingers deep within Zara's core, twisting them around to ensure she hit a certain spot. Zara's pussy clamped down on Marley's fingers. She continued to pull them back and thrust them deep, finger fucking her while she was relentless on Zara's clit.

"Marley...Marley...Marley!"

Zara's body trembled, and Marley refused to let up. She withdrew her fingers from Zara and used both hands to push Zara's legs back wide. She knelt on the bed, keeping her mouth and tongue buried deep within Zara's pussy.

Zara's muscles tightened beneath Marley's hands while she let out a bellowing scream. Zara's release gushed from her slit. Marley lapped it all up, not wanting to waste any of it.

Zara's body went limp. Marley took one more swipe with her tongue to ensure she cleaned her properly and sat back to find Zara passed out cold.

She smiled as she freed Zara's legs. Her animal was pleased she was the cause of Zara's hard orgasm that put her straight to sleep. She shifted her body to the side of the small bed and pulled Zara into her arms.

Her wolf was finally content.

CHAPTER SEVEN

Zara opened her eyes and felt safe in Marley's arms. The memory of Marley making her climax would be forever ingrained in her mind. She'd never had an orgasm like that—ever. Marley's talented tongue and fingers were amazing. She moved slightly, and Marley's arm tightened around her.

She smiled, unashamed of what had commenced between the two of them. She'd never been with a woman before, and if she had to choose her first female sexual experience, she'd choose Marley in a heartbeat.

She bit her lip, knowing Marley hadn't gotten to find release. Zara had never been a selfish lover in the past. She may not have been with a woman, but she was a quick study. She'd masturbated countless times and had given oral to her previous boyfriends. She was very proficient at sucking cock, and her exboyfriends had all loved her for it. She could figure out how to bring pleasure to Marley.

She flickered her eyes to the small window that revealed daylight was coming. She didn't know what time it was, but it seemed early. She glanced down at Marley's breasts, finding them uncovered. The cold air had her nipples beading up in tight little buds. She shifted up on her elbow, no longer able to resist.

Zara leaned over and enclosed her lips around the bud. She flicked it with her tongue. It was just as she'd figured. Even though the nipple was drawn taut, the skin was soft and pliable with her tongue.

Marley groaned when Zara twirled the nipple in her mouth.

"Good morning, Zara," Marley breathed, entwining her fingers in Zara's hair. "What are you doing?"

"I want you."

Marley's eyes snapped to hers. She nodded as Zara rolled and straddled her body. Her bare pussy brushed against Marley's abdomen.

"I'm all yours, Zara. Always have been."

Zara paused at her words. She reached out and

cupped Marley's firm breasts, loving the feel of their heaviness. She ran her hands along them, pinching the nipples and tugging them slightly. The quick intake of breath from Marley encouraged her to continue her exploration.

"Really?"

"My body is yours to do whatever you want with," Marley uttered, her eyes locked on Zara.

Zara could read the truth in them. She kneeled between Marley's legs and settled into the valley of her thighs. She took her time suckling each of Marley's round globes. She teased and fondled Marley's soft mounds before moving lower.

Nervousness filled her. She didn't want her first time pleasuring Marley to be subpar. She slid her hands along Marley's firm body while she trailed kisses across her stomach. She roamed her hand over Marley's soft skin, following the natural curve of her body. Just the feel and scent of Marley was enough to arouse Zara.

"Zara, come here," Marley whispered, motioning for her.

"No, I want to learn to please you as you did me." She shook her head.

"Let's do each other at the same time," Marley suggested. "If you want to learn, it will help you."

Zara's core clenched just at the thought of them in that particular position. She nodded and let Marley tug her toward her. Marley gripped her chin and slammed her mouth on hers.

Zara groaned and opened her mouth. This time, she wasn't going to be shy. She returned the kiss with as much fierceness as Marley gave. Her breaths came in short gasps as Marley pulled away.

"Now put your pussy on my face," Marley growled.

The glint in Marley's eyes took Zara's breath away. She didn't know what it was, but the sound of Marley's voice was slightly deeper, as if she was commanding her.

Zara liked it.

She hastily positioned herself how Marley had commanded with her pussy directly over her face. Her skin was on fire while she waited in anticipation of feeling the sensation of Marley's tongue diving deep between her now soaked folds.

Marley spread her legs wide, presenting herself to Zara. She licked her lips at the sight of Marley's arousal on her labia. Zara had always believed a woman's body was beautiful, but now being this close to Marley's pussy, Zara was anxious to discover all there was to her.

Zara moaned as Marley dove in between her folds. She lowered her head and licked Marley's pussy, replicating Marley's motion. The taste of her lover exploded on her tongue. She groaned, loving Marley's essence.

No longer shy, she gave herself over to the pleasure of Marley's tongue while determined to do the same for Marley. The sounds of their coupling filled the air. Zara introduced her fingers deep within Marley's core. Her digits were coated with Marley's arousal while she used her thumb to apply pressure to the swollen nub.

Marley was a patient teacher, allowing her to explore every facet of her pussy. Zara spread Marley's folds wide, displaying her slick clitoris and honey that poured out of her. She ran her tongue along the full length of Marley, trying to gather all of her slickness. Her whole face was submerged between Marley's legs while she explored all there was of her.

"Yes," she hissed.

Marley latched on to her clit. Zara thrust her pelvis forward, setting her own rhythm. Her hips moved on their own as she rode Marley's tongue. She duplicated the action and closed her lips around Marley's clitoris. She hummed her pleasure, gripping

Marley's thighs with her hands, leaving her face buried. Her lips were covered in the evidence of Marley's arousal.

She was loving every moment of it.

Marley spread Zara's ass cheeks wide, running her fingers along Zara's entire pussy and circling her puckered entrance.

"Keep going, Zara," Marley called out. "Yes, little one, feast on my pussy."

Marley's words urged her on while she slipped a single finger deep into Zara's forbidden hole.

"Oh God!" Zara whimpered, brushing her lips against Marley's slick folds before filling her mouth with more of Marley's honey. She used her tongue to lap up as much as she could while concentrating once again on the little bundle of nerves as Marley's finger continued to thrust deep within her ass.

Marley returned the favor, and they writhed against each other. Zara was determined to make Marley orgasm. The gasps and moans echoing through the air escalated into screams and shouts as they reached their climax together.

Zara lifted her head, gasping for breath. She panted, still amazed at the force of her release.

"Come to me, Zara," Marley commanded.

Zara immediately shifted her body at the deep

huskiness in Marley's voice. She instantly crawled up to Marley and settled into the crook of her arm.

She gazed up into Marley's eyes, the tip of Marley's fingers resting on her chin.

"Did I please you?" Zara asked, wanting to know. Deep inside, she truly was curious if Marley was satisfied with her oral performance. It was her first time, and after reaching two powerful orgasms with the woman she'd considered her best friend all these years, it wouldn't be her last attempt.

"Yes, and there is much for you to learn."

"Please, teach me."

"Do you think you can fix it?" Zara called out from above.

They'd spent the first few hours wrapped up in each other before tackling the day. Marley could still taste Zara on her tongue and hear her gasps and moans. Zara was a fast and eager learner. Marley's wolf, the daughter of the alpha, was powerful and wanted to not only claim Zara, but dominate her. She'd had to pull back quiet a few times, not wanting to scare Zara. Marley knew from their longtime friendship that Zara had only dated humans. A relationship with a shifter was totally different.

Marley pinched the bridge of her nose, staring at the engine. It was completely fried. The yacht had undergone a complete inspection before they had arrived, and all of the reports were favorable.

She crawled out of the hull and stood straight. Zara's concerned eyes met hers. She had every right to be concerned. They had no working engine. No electricity.

They were literally floating in the middle of the Pacific Ocean.

"I'm sure it could be fixed, but it won't be by me at this point," Marley breathed. She ran a shaky hand through her hair as she turned and stood staring out at the beautiful sky.

Mother Nature was a bitch. Just yesterday, she'd thrown her weight around in the way of the storm, and now today, it was beautiful sunny skies.

"Now what?"

"We send out another distress signal. There's no telling if it is being sent out. I don't know if the lightning strike damaged the radio."

"What about the flare gun?"

Marley shook her head and turned to Zara. "It would only help if someone was near to give them an idea of where we are. We need to save them until we have a reason to use them."

Zara's shoulders slumped. Marley's wolf whined, edging her forward. She walked up the few stairs up to where Zara stood. Marley gripped her chin in her hands and forced Zara's face up to meet her gaze.

"A damaged engine is not an emergency for the coast guard. This is urgent, but not an emergency. The boat is in still good floating condition, and we have food. We're safe."

"But—"

"We're going to be fine. Think positive," Marley murmured.

Zara nodded, her eyes wide with fear. Marley didn't like the thought of Zara being scared. She leaned down and laid a soft kiss to her lips.

She couldn't keep her hands off Zara. Now they had finally crossed the line from friends to lovers, Zara wouldn't know what hit her. Marley had waited years for this, and she would make the most of it.

Mate her, her wolf snapped.

Not now, she growled back to her wolf. They were nowhere near ready for that conversation. It would come in due time. This turn in their relationship was new, and Marley wanted to nurture it.

Zara leaned against her with a sigh and wrapped an arm around Marley's waist.

"I trust you, Marley. I know you'll take care of me," Zara admitted.

Marley's wolf released a howl in her chest at her words.

CHAPTER EIGHT

Z ara awoke to silence. She sat up in the bed in her cabin. They had decided to sleep together in the master suite since it offered a little more room than the one that had been Marley's. She ran her hand along Marley's side, finding it cold.

She smiled, feeling a sense of completeness and joy. Even though they were currently floating in the middle of nowhere, it gave her time to reflect on her and Marley's relationship. She sighed, thinking of all the wasted time that had passed. If only she'd had her eyes opened in the past, she would have seen what was before her.

Marley loved her.

Not just loving her as a friend, but truly loved her.

ARIEL MARIE

It all made sense now.

Zara stood from the bed and walked to the bathroom. They had to conserve water, so she quickly took care of business. Last night, they'd washed up together to save water, and it had turned very interesting. They had fallen into the bed in a tangle of arms and legs, pleasuring each other into the wee hours of the morning.

It had been almost a week since the storm. After all this time, Zara didn't believe the radio worked. No one answered, but Marley didn't want to give up. But every morning, Marley went over to the radio and sent out her urgent signal in hopes today would be the day someone would respond.

Zara stepped back out into the bedroom and went over to the small closet, finding a thin white robe. She put it on, covering her naked form, and put a loose knot in the ties. She left the cabin in search of Marley.

There was no sign of her on the main level. She must be up on the sundeck. Zara took the stairs, combing her fingers through her hair. She arrived on the deck and laughed at the sight that greeted her.

A large black wolf sat basking in the sun. Marley's face was raised as if she was absorbing the sun's rays. The animal turned her head and smiled a wolfish grin.

Marley's personality shone through the eyes locked on Zara.

She grabbed a towel hanging from the railing and made her way to the deck. She laid the towel down and sat on top of it. Marley moved over to her and placed her large head on Zara's lap.

"You are such a beauty," Zara murmured, scratching Marley's ears. Marley let out a whine when Zara pulled back her hand. The wolf butted her chest with its large head, begging for more rubs. "Oh, guess I wasn't done, huh?"

She laughed, relaxing with the black wolf lying on her. What a sight they must make. If anyone floated by now, seeing a woman sitting on the deck of a boat with a large beast would send them running away instead of rescuing them.

"What are we going to do?" she asked. It was a rhetorical question. Marley would be unable to answer her in her wolf form. Zara knew what she'd say anyway. *We wait it out. Someone will find us.*

Marley raised her head and licked Zara's cheek. She laughed as the wolf tried to repeat the motion, but Zara dodged her tongue. Marley, not having it, stood and forced Zara to accept her wolf kisses.

"Okay!" Zara giggled while Marley's wolf licked her cheeks and chin. "Heel!"

Marley paused, her mouth in that wolfish grin of hers. Merriment glinted in her blue eyes. Zara had always enjoyed spending time with Marley in her wolf form. She'd been honored multiple times to witness her pack gather for a pack run. She, of course, didn't run with them, but it was a magnificent sight to see the hundreds of wolves gather.

Marley stepped forward and placed her head against Zara's. They rested their heads together, while Zara reached up and stroked Marley's thick coat.

"When we get home, our lives will be different," Zara whispered. She pulled back and continued to run her hand along Marley's fur. Their eyes met, and Zara knew she would be returning home with hers wide open.

"Today we are going to have to empty the rainwater reservoir," Marley announced, spinning around in her captain's chair.

It had been a few days since she and Zara had hung out on the deck while she'd been in her wolf form. She'd been studying maps, and from the looks of it, they should be coming upon an island. Excitement grew in her chest, and she hoped it was a privately-owned island with humans or some way they could radio for help.

"It rained a little last night, so we may have more in it," Zara murmured, not looking up from writing in her notebook. Without electricity, she couldn't use her laptop. Even if she booted it up, they had no Wi-Fi and wouldn't be able to connect to anything, so she'd resorted to writing in a notebook.

Marley wouldn't say anything about the island quite yet until she was one hundred percent sure her calculations were correct.

They had a water purifier on board and it helped them conserve water. They'd even used the fishing rods and caught some fish. The gas top still worked with the help of a match. They had to save the gas they had left and tried not to cook with it every day.

"How's the writing coming?" she asked, eyeing Zara. She watched her set her pen down and stretch. Zara was clearly unaware of the way Marley was observing her every move.

"As well as it can be with me having to do everything by hand. I'm just plotting and hitting major points for now. Once we get home, I'll be able to type everything up. It's been a while since I've had to work on my book and not use a computer."

The boat gave a lunge, tilting on the side for a brief second before it settled back down.

"What the hell was that?" Marley muttered. She stood from her chair, her animal pacing beneath her skin. She moved to the stairs, seeing Zara stand. "Stay here."

She ran up the stairs and paused on the deck. The sun was low, denoting it was late afternoon. The warm breeze blew, lifting her hair from her neck. She strode around the deck and paused seeing what had bumped into the side of the yacht.

"Zara! Come up here," she called out, wanting to share her discovery with her lover.

"What is it?" Zara asked, curiosity brimming in her emerald eyes.

Marley motioned for her to come to her side. She entwined their fingers as she pointed out at the ocean.

"Look," she murmured.

Zara stared off in the direction, and she gasped.

Out in the ocean was a humpback whale and her calf. The boat must have been in the way of them rising to the surface for air.

"Oh my. They are beautiful," Zara exclaimed, squeezing Marley's fingers.

She leaned her head on Marley, who rested her arm on Zara's shoulders, cradling her close.

Marley's gaze was locked on the whale and baby as they swam together. The boat was no longer in danger of being tipped over by the whales, but that had been close. Instead of a bump, the size of the whale could have capsized their small vessel.

The warm breeze was comforting. Zara turned to her and raised her face to Marley's. She leaned down and captured her lips with hers, pushing her tongue into Zara's mouth. Their kiss deepened, while Zara reached up with both arms and locked her hands behind Marley's neck.

Marley tore her mouth from Zara and stared into her eyes.

Her breaths were coming fast. She slid her hands down to the curve of Zara's ass. She gripped it tight, pulling her closer. Their breasts pushed up against each other. She released a growl at Zara's giggle.

"What's so funny?" she snarled.

"I was just thinking of the day where I couldn't look away from your naked breasts and imagining what it would feel like to rub mine on yours," she admitted.

"Really? So you were checking out my tits?" She chuckled, pinching the flesh of Zara's ass, sending her into a fit of giggles.

"Yes, but now I know exactly what they taste and feel like." A sensual grin spread across her face. She raised up on tiptoe and laid a kiss on Marley's lips. "I'm going to go down and see what I can make for dinner." She placed a kiss on Marley's chin before she pulled back and walked toward the stairs.

Marley's gaze followed her curvy frame hidden by a short summer dress until she disappeared from sight.

Marley leaned against the rail and continued staring out at the whales and became lost in her thoughts. She wasn't even sure if she'd want to be rescued at this time. What was between her and Zara was perfect. Going back to the real world would change everything.

CHAPTER NINE

Marley put the last dish away in the cabinet in the kitchenette. Thanks to their water purifier, she was able to wash dishes in clean water. They'd had the perfect evening together. She finished wiping down the tiny counter before turning toward Zara who was lounging on the couch with her notebook and highlighter in her hand.

She took in the love of her life. Zara was the epitome of perfection. Her thin summer dress drew up her thighs, showing the creamy tan skin.

Her animal slammed against her chest.

Mine, her wolf snapped.

It wanted to claim Zara. She had been fighting her beast for days now, but today would not be the day her animal would break free on her.

She gripped the counter tight, watching Zara shift on the couch. She leaned over to reach for her highlighter that hit the floor and rolled away out of her grasp.

Marley's animal rose to the surface. Her breaths raced as her gaze locked on Zara who knelt on the floor searching for the marker.

Moisture collected at the apex of Marley's thighs with the sight of Zara on her knees. Her wolf stood to attention, her sights set on Zara. It was the alpha in her who wanted Zara on her knees in front of her. She was the stronger of the two, and the animal in her needed Zara to submit fully to her.

"Zara," she murmured. Her skin tingled when Zara's eyes met hers. She was battling her beast, trying to force her to settle down. "Come to me."

Her voice grew husky and dropped low with her command. Her wolf picked up the scent of Zara's arousal and let loose a howl.

Someone liked to be ordered around.

She filed that away in the back of her mind for later. Zara moved to stand, but Marley held up her hand.

"Stay down on your knees and come to me." Her voice held a hint of a growl as she fought an internal battle with her wolf. Zara's delicious scent grew stronger. She did as she was told and stayed on all fours, crawling toward Marley. Her emerald eyes darkened with lust. She stopped before Marley and shifted to her knees. Marley extended a hand and gripped her chin, running her thumb along Zara's plump bottom lip.

"Take my shorts off, Zara."

Without a word, Zara reached up and gripped Marley's cotton shorts and tugged them down, sliding them to the floor.

Marley kicked them away and widened her stance. Her pussy was pulsating, needing to feel Zara's tongue deep within her folds. In the past couple weeks, Zara had quickly learned the art of eating pussy and had mastered it.

If she didn't know any better, she'd say Zara was addicted to it.

Her eyes turned back to Marley who smiled at her mate.

"You know what I need, Zara."

Zara opened her mouth wide and covered Marley's pussy. Marley released a hiss at the feeling of Zara's tongue parting her slit. She leaned back against the counter while Zara slowly ran her tongue along her slick folds.

"Is this what you needed?" Zara asked. Her voice was muffled as her tongue probed deeper.

"Yes," she groaned, reaching down with her hand and threading her fingers in Zara's blonde locks.

She anchored Zara's head in place, thrusting her pussy along her mate's tongue. Their eyes locked while Zara continued her sensual consumption of Marley. Only her eyes were visible, but that was all Marley needed.

Her breaths came faster. Zara latched on to her sensitive nub and sucked on it with great force. Marley's knees grew weak, and as if sensing this, Zara placed her hands on the backs of Marley's thighs for leverage. Her head shook back and forth while she hummed, sending a vibration through Marley's drenched core.

"Harder. Suck my clit harder," she growled, commanding her lover in the way she needed to be pleased. Her animal paced, wanting to be in control of Zara, dominate her and prove to her she was an alpha wolf and would protect her, cherish her, and love her forever.

She cried out as the pressure increased on her bundle of nerves. She thrust her hips and swirled them around, heightening her pleasure. Her nipples painfully pushed at her shirt, and she ripped it off completely, freeing her sensitive mounds.

Zara pushed her legs open. Marley glanced at the counter ledge that stuck out to divide the kitchen from the dining room. She lifted her leg and balanced her foot on the edge of the counter, opening herself fully for Zara.

Zara immediately slid her fingers deep inside her slick channel, finger fucking her while she continued to suck and pull on her clitoris.

"Yes, Zara. Take your fill of my pussy," she shouted. Her release slammed into her, and she released a growl. Her body shook from the sensations coursing through her. She placed her foot on the floor while Zara sat back with a pleased look on her face. Her mouth was coated with the evidence of Marley's release.

"Are you satisfied, my love?" Zara asked.

With a growl, Marley pulled Zara to her feet and immediately took her dress off. Pleased she was naked beneath it, Marley pushed her toward the table and bent her over it.

"Very pleased." Her reply was short and curt because she had one thing on her mind. Tasting her mate and making her come. "Hold on to the table and spread your legs as wide as you can."

Zara followed her orders without complaint. Marley knelt behind her, finding the scent of her arousal strong. She leaned forward and nipped Zara's ass cheek with her incisors. Zara jumped and gasped. She bathed the area with her tongue to soothe it.

"Marley," Zara moaned, her body wriggling on the table.

Marley spread Zara's ass cheeks far apart, revealing her pretty puckered anus. She licked the forbidden hole before trailing it down to Zara's slick core. She loved every part of the woman spread out in front of her.

Anything Marley wanted to try, Zara was ready and willing.

Zara cried out from Marley's assault on her. Her breasts were crushed on the table while Marley made a meal out of her ass and slick pussy. Her legs shook from her orgasm rushing toward her.

She thrust her ass back to Marley as she currently was bathing Zara's forbidden hole with her tongue. She moaned, feeling Marley's fingers slip deep with in her ass and another finger inside her slick core.

"Your body is perfect for me," Marley admitted, her voice breathless. "I can never tell what part I want."

"God, take all of me," Zara whimpered, loving the sensation of her fingers thrusting harder into her. She slid her own hand down to her folds, needing a release. Her fingers met her drenched clit, and she rubbed it.

"Yes, play with yourself. Come on my tongue," Marley ordered.

Zara's juices flowed out of her even faster at Marley's husky command. Something about the way Marley ordered her around had her painfully aroused and wanting to please the shifter in any and every way she possibly could.

Her cries filled the air when she finally found her release. Her scream started deep within her chest before it ripped its way out of her. It was long and drawn out. The waves of her orgasm swept through her body.

She slumped on the table, spent from the excessive use of energy. She closed her eyes and laid still, unable to move. She lost track of how long she laid there, but a sensation greeted her.

She smiled, Marley trailing soft kisses from her ass up and along her spine. Her lover pulled her from the table and lifted her. Zara wrapped her arms around Marley's neck while being carried over to the couch. Marley sat and placed Zara on her lap with her legs straddling her.

Zara opened her eyes and found Marley gazing at her with nothing but love on her face.

"Hey." Zara smiled, brushing the dark hair from Marley's face. She leaned in, covering Marley's mouth with hers. She poured all of her feelings for her into the kiss. The last few weeks they'd been stuck out in the ocean had made her realize one thing.

She loved Marley.

Not in best friend fashion. No, she was *in* love with her. She couldn't see herself with any other person.

She pulled back and rested her head on Marley's.

Marley tugged her closer to her where Zara's pussy rested on her stomach.

"Hey," Marley replied.

The predator gleam was in her eyes, and it sent a shiver down Zara's spine. She wrapped her arms tight around Marley's neck, not afraid of her. She knew Marley would never hurt her in a million years.

"We need to talk," Marley said.

"About what?" Zara asked. It was going to be hard to concentrate, and she prayed it wasn't something serious. One orgasm wouldn't do. Her body was becoming well-trained to multiple releases back to back when Marley made love to her, and tonight she didn't want it to be any different.

"Us."

Zara smiled and trailed her fingers down Marley's face. Her eyes were intense as she gazed at Zara.

"I thought we established the first night we began sharing a cabin that there would be an us?"

"Yes, while we are alone. But once we get back to the real world, what will your family think of us? Shifters accept same-sex couples with no issues because we know it is fate who decides our mate."

Zara paused and stared at Marley. She bit her lip, gazing into Marley's beautiful, clear-blue eyes.

"Are you saying what I think you are saying?"

"You're my mate, Zara. Always have been. I didn't know if you would accept me or not, so I chose the route of friendship. I would have rather had you as a friend and be in my life than to be rejected."

Zara's sight became blurred as tears pooled in her eyes.

"Why are you just now telling me this?"

"This time we've shared on this boat in the middle of nowhere has been a dream come true. But I know eventually we will get rescued and we'll be back in the real world. So no matter what happens, I wanted you to know you were a gift from fate. I'll always cherish this time we've had together."

Marley reached out her hand and wiped the tears rolling down Zara's cheeks.

"That is the most beautiful thing anyone has ever said to me." Her voice cracked.

Marley pulled her into a tight embrace. When they got back home, nothing was going to change. Damn the world, she'd always known they were meant to be together.

CHAPTER TEN

Zara let loose a sigh as she lay cradled in Marley's arms. The cabin was basked in darkness while they rested in the bed listening to the sounds of the ocean surrounding the vessel.

"Do you think our families are missing us?" Zara whispered, not wanting to disturb their comfortable silence. Her naked body was pressed against Marley's. Tonight, they'd both fallen into the bed, tired from a long day. Their days were beginning to run into each other as each one passed.

Marley's fingers lazily drew circles on her lower back, awakening Zara's desires. She bit her lip, trying to push her libido down. She was interested in hearing Marley's response.

"By now they should know something is wrong,"

Marley replied, her soft voice breaking through the air.

Her hand slid across the supple skin of Zara's back, sending a shiver down Zara's spine.

"We would have checked in once we'd arrived at Tahiti. I'm sure my father is scouring the waters for us by now. He won't stop until he finds us or our..."

Zara closed her eyes tight at the dreadful thought. There was no way they could die out here. She prayed it would never happen. She had faith in Evan Gerwulf. He was a powerful alpha who would move Heaven or Earth to protect his only daughter.

"If you were home right now, what would you want to do?" Zara asked, changing the subject.

"Well, at the moment, a long, hot shower." Marley giggled.

Zara chuckled, thinking that would be her answer, too. They'd barely been able to wash since they had to conserve water on the boat. It truly helped to have the water purifier on board so they could trap rainwater and clean it for them to use. Bathing in the sink wasn't ideal, but at least it was something.

"I'd vote for the jacuzzi tub you have in your bathroom," Zara murmured, imagining being able to soak in a bath, thinking of all the times she had taken thoroughly washing herself for granted. Back home, Zara had always teased Marley for the oversized tub she had in her master bathroom. It could fit at least four to five people. Now she would give anything to be able to soak in it.

"What? As much as you teased me about it?" Marley laughed, pulling Zara closer to her, crushing her breasts between them.

"Who would have thought, right?" Zara smiled against Marley's collarbone. She reached over and laid her hand on Marley's flat abdomen.

"What books are you working on? I know that brain of yours is rolling a mile a minute and coming up with new ideas." Marley dropped a gentle kiss on Zara's forehead.

Zara loved just resting in the bed talking with Marley. This was no different than all of the years they'd been friends and had talked for hours. They even had girls' nights and stayed at each other's homes just to lie around, drink wine, and watch movies all night.

How did she not know the connection with Marley was on this level? She rubbed her thumb against the soft ridge of Marley's belly.

"Well, since I don't have my computer to write, I've been plotting. It's been a while since I've just used pen and paper. It's like back in high school when I wrote my first book."

"I remember that. It was a high school drama," Marley murmured.

"It wasn't my best work at all." Zara shook her head. No, it wasn't. She cringed thinking of her first novel. It was a young adult romantic suspense based around a murder that took place on the school grounds. It followed four seniors who were friends, and the enemy of one of the females was found dead in the school's swimming pool.

"Hey, it opened the doors to your success now. You are currently one of the hottest writers of this time. Your books fly off the shelves the minute you release them. Think if you had not written the first book, you might be doing something else right now."

Zara smiled. Marley was always her biggest supporter. When her parents had scoffed at the idea of her using her degree in English to become a romance author, Marley had been right there with her. Her parents had hoped she'd work as a teacher, but Zara had always had dreams of bringing the characters floating around in her head to life and sharing them with the world.

She continued to stroke Marley's soft skin while

drifting lower. She stopped at her navel, dipping into the little alcove of her stomach.

"When did you know?" Zara asked. Her heart skipped a beat at the magnitude of the question. She wanted to know how long she had been blind to the true nature of Marley's feelings for her.

"You remember the day when we were in swim class and everyone was rushing out of the showers to get dressed and you slipped and fell?"

Zara paused her hand. That had been the day they'd met. Their sophomore year in high school. She remembered it as if it were yesterday. One didn't forget the day they'd met their best friend who'd stuck by their side through thick and thin.

Their teacher had announced there would be a fire drill, and everyone was to hurry up and go to their next class so they wouldn't be still trying to get dressed during the drill. The girls had scurried past, and Zara had wanted to finish rinsing the shampoo from her hair. She'd caught the eyes of a young girl with dark hair who was taller than most at their age.

She'd instantly recognized her as a shifter. Zara had smiled at her and nodded before turning. Zara had gone to jog out of the open shower when her foot slipped. She'd landed on her knees, hard, bruising them. The dark-haired girl had come over and helped her up. A smile and a laugh later, they'd become instant friends.

"I had just turned sixteen," Zara whispered in awe. Her heart pounded with the information.

Marley stroked Zara's hair.

"Me, too," Marley replied.

Their birthdays were a week apart, and they had celebrated it together every year since.

Zara caressed Marley's stomach again as more questions came to mind. She slowly continued its descent lower.

"Does your family know your wolf identified me as your mate?"

"Yes, from the moment I met you, I told them."

Marley released a deep breath when Zara slid her hand along her mons pubis. Her chest rumbled with a low growl. Zara smiled, recognizing the signs Marley's wolf was nearing the surface and wanted to make her presence known. Zara's hand connected with the smooth, bare skin.

"And what did your parents think?"

She was deliberately torturing Marley while they spoke. She couldn't help it. When they were this close and naked, sex was never far from her mind, but right now she wanted to tease her lover while they had their conversation. She slid her fingers softly over Marley's swollen nub peeking out from between her labia.

"They were accepting." Marley groaned, her legs widening, inviting Zara's hand to move farther down.

Zara's breaths were increasing as she grew aroused, but she wanted to continue their conversation.

"Really?"

"You know shifters love who they love, and mate with who they are fated to be with. Human society was built on the assumption it should be a man and a woman. Shifters began to celebrate when humans followed suit and fell in love with who they wanted."

Zara slipped her finger between the moist folds of her lover, knowing Marley was right. Society was finally accepting of same-sex couples. She thought of her parents and if they would accept her newfound relationship with Marley. Her parents already loved Marley like a daughter. The girls had been glued to the hip since they were sixteen.

Her parents loved her unconditionally, and she was sure they would be accepting that Zara and Marley's relationship had blossomed into much more.

"When we get back home, will there be an 'us' still?" Zara whispered, needing to know. She was playing dirty asking the question while her fingers were buried inside Marley.

She watched Marley's body tremble as she widened her legs. Her pelvis rocked against Zara's hands. Her back arched off the bed, putting her breasts eye level with Zara who leaned forward and captured the one closest to her. She sucked the mound deep within her mouth, flicking the taut nipple with her tongue.

Marley's response was a gasp. She tightened her grip in Zara's hair.

She quickened her motion on Marley's clit and pulled back away from her tit.

"Marley, what's my answer? I need to know." She licked the titty, unable to get enough of the taste of Marley's skin.

She wanted Marley to tell her what she wanted to hear. She had made up her mind there would be no one else for her. If she was Marley's mate, then she'd honor that and do what she'd need to do in order to make it permanent between the two of them.

"You're mine," Marley growled through clenched teeth. "Now put your mouth on my pussy and make me come."

Zara's pussy pulsated with the command. The

dominance of Marley's animal was a huge turn on, and her anticipation grew with the knowledge she had a lifetime to look forward to of being dominated. She moved her body lower on the bed between Marley's legs, pushing them far apart.

"Yes, mate. As you wish." She licked the entire length of Marley's slit before closing her mouth around her clitoris. She stopped her questions and proceeded to do as she was told.

CHAPTER ELEVEN

"Do you really think someone will locate us?"

Marley turned to find Zara standing at the entryway to the living room. Marley placed the receiver down, having just sent out another call on the transmitter radio. Every day she put out a call in hopes someone would hear her, but each time no one answered. A sigh escaped her as she stared out the window at the bright, early morning sky.

Her shoulders slumped. She was unsure of how to answer Zara. Her ears picked up the soft padding of Zara's bare feet crossing the room. Soft hands settled on her shoulders, pulling her around to face Zara.

Marley took in Zara's curvy frame covered by her thin white robe that did nothing to hide her nipples pressed against the soft material. Marley reached out and undid the ties. There was no point in her covering herself walking around the boat. The robed puddled on the floor, leaving Zara naked. Her body was soft and held curves in all the right spots. Her full breasts with their dusky rose areolae drove Marley crazy. She tugged Zara to her, resting her head on Zara's belly.

"I don't know. I held out hope someone would find us," Marley whispered, her heart sinking with the thought they may not be found. The ocean was a vast part of the continent, and the chance of them being rescued lessened with each passing day.

Zara's fingers threaded their way into Marley's hair. A slight tug brought Marley's head back, forcing her to stare into Zara's eyes. She straddled Marley's lap, holding Marley's head back so she could lay a small kiss on her lips. Her lips lingered first, pressing hard against Marley's. Their kiss was intense and deep. Marley controlled the kiss, gripping Zara's ass in her hands while tilting her head. Their tongues dueled briefly before they both pulled back, out of breath.

"We can't give up hope. You said fate brought me into your life and I'm the one for you. Do you want to know what I believe?" Zara's emerald eyes deepened.

A shiver slid down Marley's spine. She was captivated by Zara, unable to look away. She slowly caressed the supple skin of Zara's ass, holding her in place.

They'd made love almost every night, and still Marley couldn't get enough of Zara. With her being a wolf, her sexual appetite was voracious, and so far, Zara was able to keep up with her, confirming she was Marley's mate.

"What is that?" she asked, her voice just a soft whisper.

"I believe fate put me in your life for a reason, and there is no way in hell our story is going to be cut short on this boat. We will have a future." Zara leaned her head down and rested it on Marley's.

Marley's heart swelled, filled with love for the woman in front of her. Her wolf whined, pacing as if to alert her. Her ears pricked up, and she pulled back from Zara.

"What is it?" Zara asked.

Marley stood and set Zara on her feet. She brushed past Zara, heading for the stairs to the upper deck. Her wolf growled once she emerged from below. The waters were calm for a change. She walked around the boat and froze in place.

She couldn't believe it.

They were floating past land.

The island from the map!

"Zara!" she shouted, running toward the captain's wheel. She sat in the chair and reached under into the cabinet below and grabbed her binoculars.

She used the device; it assisted her shifter vision in seeing the island.

"What's going on?" Zara asked, appearing at the top of the stairs, putting her robe back on, but she left the ties open. Her soft skin peeked from in between the opening as she came to stand beside her.

"Look, over there." Marley pointed, handing the binoculars to her.

"Oh my goodness. Is that an island? Are there people on it?" she exclaimed, jumping in place.

"I don't know. I think we should try to get to it," Marley suggested, facing Zara.

"Do you think it's safe?"

"I don't know, but it will get us off this boat," she replied. She would have to admit she was suffering a bit of cabin fever. Not that she didn't love spending the days on the boat with Zara, but it would be nice to stretch her animal legs and run around a sandy beach.

Her gaze met the excited eyes of Zara, who held a wide grin on her face.

"Let's do it."

Marley laughed and stood. "We can drop the anchor and use the emergency raft to get over there."

"We should pack some supplies," Zara blurted out. She turned and ran back down below.

Marley turned and let out a curse. This would be the perfect time for the computer to miraculously flip back on, but there was no such luck. She stood and ran toward the stern and took the stairs down to the swim deck and opened the compartment for the anchor.

With her shifter strength, it was easy for her to pull the anchor out of the storage compartment and lower it into the water. The chain continued to extend until it couldn't move anymore. She stood and waited, watching the boat's rate slow down. Soon they were anchored to the ocean bed and were no longer floating away. She looked in the direction and could have shouted for joy at the short distance to the island.

They would take the lifeboat and row their way

to land. Once they arrived, she would shift to her animal in order to check for danger.

She narrowed her eyes on the island and sent up a small prayer they wouldn't run into any danger.

———————

Zara flew around the bedroom packing clothes. It would be exciting to finally get off the boat. They wouldn't be saved and on their way home, but at least they'd be on solid ground. She threw on a pair of shorts and a bikini top since the air was so humid. She was glad she'd brought so many swimsuits with the heat on the boat growing to unbearable temperatures during the day. She grabbed her bag and went up the stairs to find Marley.

"I have the lifeboat ready to go," Marley announced when Zara arrived at her side. They'd worked for the past hour gathering things they would need on land. "What if it's not inhabited?"

"Then we can camp out at least on dry land. This boat was stocked with all the essentials. I have a tent we can use. Once we've found a safe spot, I'll shift and explore it. My wolf will pick up scents of animals and if there are any humans around. My nose is stronger when I'm in my animal form."

Zara nodded and followed Marley to the swim deck where the lifeboat was tethered to the yacht. Marley helped her on it and took the bags she'd packed and stored them in the front of the small emergency boat. Zara turned to the yacht, slightly relieved to get off it, but yet it held so many memories she was a slightly sad to be leaving their little love cove.

Marley settled on the boat and untied them from the yacht. She reached for the oars and began the slow trip to the island.

"It looks beautiful," Zara said, shading her eyes with her hand. She took in the island as it they got closer. Thankfully, with Marley's shifter strength, she wasn't tiring.

"An island in the middle of the Pacific Ocean would have to be." Marley chuckled, getting into a rhythm with her strokes.

Anticipation grew in Zara's chest as they made the trip. She fell silent, not wanting to distract Marley from getting them to safety. She was a nervous being this far out in the ocean in an even smaller vessel than the yacht. She turned her head and was barely able to make out the name of the yacht on the side.

Dream Weaver.

She smiled, thinking she had been awoken on the ship. She now looked forward to weaving her dreams into reality. Her gaze met Marley's, and her heart slammed into her chest.

Zara loved her, and she needed to find the perfect way to tell her.

Marley's tanned skin was highlighted by her pink bikini top. She, too, had chosen to wear shorts. Her hair was pulled up in a high bun, with strands escaping and blowing in the wind. Her toned muscles flexed with each movement, making Zara's breathing slow down.

She swallowed hard, knowing this was not the time for her to be getting aroused watching Marley. From what she could tell, they'd been on the boat for at least a month. She released a deep breath, readying herself for the second leg of their adventure.

CHAPTER TWELVE

"I never thought I would be appreciative of walking on land again," Zara exclaimed, twirling around in a circle. She ran a few feet away before turning back to face Marley.

Marley laughed at her mate's antics, feeling the same. She would need to shift and find a safe place for them to bunker down for the night. She wanted to ensure this island would be secured for the two of them. If not, they'd make their way back to the yacht.

"I know. It feels good to have this sand in between my toes." Marley groaned, glancing down at her feet. Sand beneath her toes was a true treat. She looked up as Zara made her way to her. She opened her arms to pull Zara into a hug.

"It's beautiful," Zara murmured, tucking her head under Marley's chin.

Marley gripped Zara in a tight hug that was returned.

"I just hope it's safe where we can stay here for a while," Zara said.

"I won't let anything happen to you," Marley promised. She tipped Zara's chin up to meet her eyes. She pressed her lips to Zara's to seal the deal. Her wolf would fight tooth and nail to ensure Zara remained unharmed.

"I know," Zara whispered, pulling back. She smiled a wide grin, reaching up and entwining her fingers behind Marley's neck. "We can turn this into our private little nude beach once you come back."

"I look forward to it," she growled playfully, squeezing Zara's plump bottom. Visions of exploring each other on the sand beneath the open skies was enough get her painfully aroused immediately.

"Good. The quicker we get work done, we can play."

Zara gave her a wink, and Marley couldn't help but grab a swift kiss again. She gripped Zara's face in her hands and thoroughly kissed her. Her nipples beaded as they pushed forth against Zara's breasts.

She tore her lips from Zara, knowing she was

right. They must work first. They would have all the time in the world later to play.

"Before settling on a spot to set up camp, let's explore and see what we find," Marley suggested.

Zara nodded and followed behind Marley. They chose the most important backpack Zara would carry while Marley was in her wolf form. They hid the rest of their things by partially burying them and covering them with loose tree branches and leaves. They even brought the lifeboat on the shore and hid it in the wood.

Satisfied everything was secured, Marley began removing her bikini top, shorts, and sandals. She glanced up and caught Zara's eyes taking her in, and she smirked. Her little human mate couldn't hide the passion in her eyes. She walked over to Zara and handed over her belongings to be stored in the backpack.

"Later," she murmured.

Zara chuckled as she stood back and waited for Marley to transform into her animal.

Marley winked and then called on her. Her wolf, having been waiting for this moment, rushed forth, sending Marley to her knees on the sand. Electricity coursed through her as her body began its transformation. Dark hair sprouted on her arms. Her bones lengthened and reshaped themselves. Her vision sharpened while she completed the change.

Finally in her wolf form, Marley shook her head and let loose a huff. She turned her gaze to Zara who stepped forward and rubbed her head.

"Lead the way," Zara urged, hefting the bag onto her back.

Marley marched toward the brush immediately, taking in all the scents and smells assaulting her sensitive nose. They walked through the woods in comfortable silence. Marley didn't sense any threats, but she remained alert. Her gaze roamed the area to ensure she remembered key landmarks so they would be able to make their way back to the beach and their belongings.

They continued on for a short while. Her wolf had finally relaxed as they walked. She had to rein her animal in. Her beast wanted to go off and give chase to the smaller animals of the island.

She paused, blinking, and looked down at the ground. The path that was not really there before was not a pronounced man-made walkway. Marley sensed humans had been here.

She glanced over her shoulder at Zara and could see she recognized it, too.

Determined, she moved forward, her attention

sharpened to listen out for the signs of humans. She kept her nose in the air, trying to pick up any new scents, but only the aroma of nature surrounded them. Their steps quickened as they followed the path. Anticipation grew for what was waiting at the end of their journey. She ached to run but couldn't leave Zara behind. Her human legs wouldn't be able to keep up with Marley's wolf sprints.

They rounded the small bend, and both froze in place at the sight that greeted them.

"Oh my," Zara gushed, reaching a hand out and rubbing Marley's head.

A wolfish grin spread across Marley's mouth.

A house.

A fucking house stood erected before them, and it was the most beautiful sight she'd seen in a while.

"Please tell me we're going to see if someone is home," Zara asked, her eyes wide with excitement.

Marley nodded, unable to respond. She set out in a trot but turned and waved a paw to Zara. Marley wanted to check out the area around the house first.

Zara seemed to understand what Marley wanted and stayed back. Marley turned and took off toward the house. She arrived near the structure and immediately sniffed out the land around it and disappeared behind it.

No one was here.

She couldn't pick up the scent of humans at all.

Her wolf shoulders slumped a little, but she was still hopeful. The house appeared to be in great shape. The property was well-manicured and looked to be a getaway retreat. Marley made her way back around to the front of the house and let loose a yip, calling for Zara.

Zara's gaze was locked on the sprawling house while she walked closer to it. It was a beautiful home made almost completely of glass. She was sure the owners wanted to capitalize on the beauty of nature and the bright sun. If it was her home on this secluded island, she would have done the same. She was anxious to explore it and prayed the electricity worked.

Marley appeared in her human form, naked from shifting.

"I don't sense any danger and I don't think anyone has been here in a while," Marley said, motioning for Zara to follow her.

They walked around the home with its beautiful and serene landscape. Zara took in the lush greenery and thicket pushed back away from the home. They came upon the back yard, finding a massive deck attached to the house.

"Wow," she gasped, assessing the dark wood and the plants decorating the stone walkway leading up to the deck's stairs.

"I found a generator and I think I may be able to get it on, and you know what that means." Marley wagged her eyebrows.

"Electricity, possibly hot water and a bath!" Zara exclaimed, skipping up the stairs. She glanced around the deck and was impressed. "This has to be someone's vacation home or secret getaway."

"That's what I was thinking. Let's keep our fingers crossed there is a phone." Marley nodded, walking up the stairs. She headed toward the double glass patio doors and turned the handle. Her gaze flew to Zara when it turned.

"There is a god," Zara whispered, watching Marley open the doors. She could have wept with relief. They wouldn't have to sleep in a tent on the beach. Hopefully this home had spare bedrooms they could borrow until they could be rescued.

They walked through the doors and found themselves in a chef's kitchen. It had all of the characteristics showing it belonged to someone who knew their way around a stove and oven.

"This is beautiful," Marley murmured, moving forward. "Stay here. I'm going to just do a quick walk through and ensure we are alone."

Zara nodded and took a seat at the large marble island situated in the center of the room. There was an attached family room and dining room off to the side.

Marley disappeared down the hallway.

Zara strained to hear but couldn't pick up any noise. Marley, ever the shifter, was light on her feet and didn't produce any sound at all. A few minutes passed by and still no sign of Marley. Zara slid from the chair and stepped down into the family room and glanced around. She didn't see any photos to show who lived here.

Artwork decorated the walls around the tastefully arranged home. She walked over to the windows and stared at the beautiful picture that nature made. She sighed, wishing they were here for just a relaxing vacation.

"It would seem we are alone." Marley's voice startled Zara.

She spun around to find her naked lover standing with her hands on her hips.

"Not sure if is a good thing or bad. Do you think you can get the generator working?"

"Yeah, I should be able to. The home is pretty much stocked with whatever we need. I didn't check the kitchen out."

"I'll do it while you check on the generator," Zara volunteered, moving back into the kitchen.

Marley disappeared out the patio doors and down the stairs. Zara focused on the kitchen, opening the cabinets and drawers.

Her heart skipped a beat at her discovery.

Dry goods and cooking utensils. She moved to the sink and turned the handle.

Running water!

Now if only they could find a phone.

The wonderful purr of electricity greeted her ears.

"Yes!" She danced around the kitchen, hopeful the rest of their trip would improve. It couldn't possibly get any worse. They'd survive a powerful storm and weeks just floating the ocean. This trip could only get better.

"And we have light," Marley announced, walking through the door.

Zara flew to her, throwing herself at Marley who caught her in midair with a laugh. She wrapped her legs around Marley and squeezed her arms tight.

"That is the best thing you've said to me all day." She laughed, planting a huge kiss on Marley's lips.

"I have something that might be even better. They have fishing poles out there, and we can go catch a couple of fish and come back here to cook a fabulous dinner."

"And then I can take a shower with hot water?" Zara asked. Her heart was racing with the positive news.

"Of course," Marley murmured, laying a kiss on Zara's lips. "We'll go fishing, come back, and you can shower while I get dinner started."

"You sure know how to treat a woman. Let's go."

CHAPTER THIRTEEN

"I don't think I can eat anymore," Zara mumbled, sitting on her lounge chair.

They had located furniture meant for the deck in a shed in the back yard. They had searched and found everything they would need to relax out on the deck under the stars. They even had citronella candles lit around to ward off the bugs and provide a little light.

Discovering the island was turning out better than Marley would have ever thought.

Marley smirked watching her mate exaggerate how full she was. Their afternoon had been wonderful but busy. They'd taken the fishing rods and followed another pathway to a pier in the ocean.

After a couple of hours they'd gone back to the house, ecstatic with their catch.

Tonight would be a night of full relaxation. They had both taken long, fulfilling showers and scrubbed themselves so they literally glowed. They had even had the chance to wash what little clothes they'd brought with them, and the items were currently hanging up on the clothing line in the yard.

While Zara had taken her shower, Marley had explored the house further. She let out a deep breath and relaxed back in her chair that was beside Zara's. Her gaze moved to the open sky and took in the stars.

"While you were in the shower, I snooped around some more in the house," Marley began. She paused, feeling Zara's eyes on her.

"And..." Zara gently urged her on.

Marley turned to Zara with a small smile on her lips. She took in the curiosity on Zara's face and knew she had to be honest. She was sure once they retuned home, their lives would definitely be changed. Already this time lost in the middle of nowhere had meant the world to Marley.

"I found a transistor radio and a satellite phone," she admitted. She nervously brushed her hair behind her ear.

Mate her, her wolf whispered.

Her hands shook with the thought. Her wolf would finally settle down when she put her mark on Zara. It would be the only way they could truly be together. Shifters were slow to age and lived long lives. With the mating bite from a shifter, an enzyme would be released into the human's blood. It would match their aging to that of a shifter, allowing them to spend a long lifespan together.

"Did you put out the call already?"

Marley shook her head. She had come to the conclusion she would ask Zara to take the final step in their relationship and mate with her. Her heart raced with the thought.

What if Zara rejected their mating?

Marley's heart would crumble if Zara refused her and her wolf.

Zara had spoken of their future together, but mating was a higher level than just being a couple. It was creating a bond that could never be broken. Sealing them for all of eternity until one of them died, and even then, their heart would still long for the other until they, too, joined their mate in the afterlife.

"I was thinking we would do it in the morning. We are safe here. Let's take this night and make the most of it. Once we're rescued, there's no—"

"I agree," Zara cut her off. Her smile widened as she turned in her chair and rested her feet on the deck. "Tonight I want you all to myself. We will put the call out at first light."

Marley smiled, loving how her mate always seemed to be on the same page as her.

"Great minds think alike," Marley noted, facing Zara.

Do it now, her wolf urged.

She swallowed hard and stood to her feet. Zara watched her, love brimming in her eyes as Marley knelt on the wooden floor before her. Even though they had yet to say the words, Marley knew deep down Zara loved her.

Marley ran her hands along Zara's smooth, exposed thighs. They were both dressed in their bikinis while their clothes hung out to dry.

Nervousness filled Marley while she met the gaze of Zara.

"What is it, love?" Zara coaxed, brushing the hair from Marley's face.

Her soft fingers slid along Marley's hairline, and a chill slid down Marley's spine.

"Mate with me," Marley breathed. It was now or never. Her eyes searched Zara's, and she waited with baited breath for an answer.

Zara smiled, nodding. She tugged Marley close and covered her mouth with hers in the most sweetest kiss Marley could imagine. The air in her lungs escaped as the kiss grew more intense. Marley reached up and threaded her fingers in Zara's hair, anchoring them together. She moved between the valley of Zara's thighs, putting their bodies flush against each other.

She drew back, needing to hear the words come from Zara's lips.

"Will you?" inquired Marley.

"Yes," Zara exclaimed, wrapping her arms around Marley. She leaned forward and rested her forehead against Marley's. "I want to spend the rest of my life with you."

"You do understand what it means to mate with a shifter, right?" Marley asked.

"Of course I do. I've only been best friends with a shifter practically my entire life. I've paid attention to what goes on in your world. You'll put your mark on me—"

She was rudely interrupted by Marley's wolf letting out a deep growl.

They both chuckled before growing serious again.

"As I was saying, I know you will put your mark

on me and then I will live a long life to be able to spend it with you," she whispered.

"Forever is a long time," Marley murmured, sliding her fingers down the small of Zara's back. She basked in the feel of their closeness. She didn't know why she'd had doubts. She should have known better. Fate had decided Zara was the one for her. She only had to be patient.

"We've already spent half our lives as friends, now we'll get to spend the rest of our lives together as mates."

Marley pulled back and gripped Zara's face with her hands, staring deep into her eyes. The moon rays streaming down on them provided just enough light.

"I love you, Zara. I always have," she admitted, her gaze on Zara.

She smiled at Marley as she untied her bikini top and let it fall to the deck. She untied both ties on her hips and removed her bottoms, leaving her naked. She shook her hair and rested her hands on the chair, presenting herself to Marley. She was the epitome of sexiness.

Marley's beast slammed against her chest.

Take her, it demanded. *Mate her.*

"I love you, too, Marley. Now make me yours."

Zara led the way into the master bedroom of their borrowed house. She tightened her hand on Marley's as she guided her into the room. Her heart was racing knowing this was the ultimate step in their relationship.

A mating was forever.

She may not be a wolf shifter, but from all the years she had spent around Marley's pack, she understood the magnitude of it.

She couldn't see herself with anyone else.

Not her ex-boyfriend, Bo, or any of the other men she'd been involved with. She truly believed this was the reason she was never satisfied with her previous relationships. She had been searching for someone who had been right in front of her the whole time.

Marley.

She let Marley's hand go so she could walk over and turn the bedroom lamp. The room faced the thick woods, its walls made of pure glass. There was an atmosphere of being at one with nature. The soft glow from the lamp helped illuminate the room just enough to allow Zara to see Marley clearly.

Her eyes met the feral gaze of Marley.

Her animal was close. It would have to be in order to place Marley's mating mark on her. Zara's core clenched in anticipation of receiving the mark. It was one that should be displayed with honor, and Zara wouldn't have a problem showing it off.

Zara lowered her gaze to the floor while she walked toward Marley in a show of submission. She held back a smirk, thinking of all the dynamics of a wolf shifter's pack. Marley was an alpha's daughter. Her and her brother, Conan, were the future of the pack and had alpha genes flowing through their blood.

Zara didn't mind being the submissive mate. She knew Marley would always treat her with respect and as an equal. Zara thought of Marley's parents and knew her mother was the submissive wolf in the relationship and Mr. Gerwulf put his mate on a pedestal. Zara hoped to have what they had.

With Marley, it was guaranteed.

Zara stopped in front of Marley, who had yet to say one word. She knelt on the floor before Marley. Her heart raced as she finally glanced up into Marley's eyes. A small smile played on Marley's lips. She reached down and caressed Zara's cheek.

"You remembered," Marley breathed, her eyes holding a pleased look.

Of course she remembered the ways of Marley's people.

Zara reached up and slid down Marley's bikini bottoms while Marley removed the top. Now they both were naked, and Zara was ready to show how much she loved her soon-to-be mate. She ran her hands along Marley's legs, starting at her ankles and moved her way up. She gently laid a kiss on Marley's thigh before doing the same to the other.

Marley's skin was smooth and tanned. She widened her stance to allow Zara to have her way. Zara's eyes were drawn to Marley's center. She leaned forward and gave one long swipe of her tongue in between Marley's slit.

"Yes," Marley hissed, reaching out and threading her fingers in Zara's hair.

Zara's gaze connected with Marley's as she covered her pussy with her mouth. Zara thrust her tongue in Marley's folds while holding on to Marley's toned legs. She took her time tasting Marley. She could spend a lifetime with her face buried in her woman's pussy. It gave her great pleasure to know she had mastered the art of making Marley come on her tongue. She had always enjoyed giving her ex-boyfriends blowjobs, but she loved eating pussy more.

Marley's body trembled while Zara concentrated on her clit. She rotated between licking and sucking on the little bundle of nerves, knowing it was driving Marley crazy. She watched Marley's head fall back when she latched on to the swollen nub.

Marley cried out, pulling Zara's head away from her core.

"No, not yet." Marley tugged Zara up from her position on the floor and turned her around, pushing her toward the bed.

A flash of fang caught Zara's attention, and her core clenched.

It was time.

CHAPTER FOURTEEN

Marley's wolf chanted the word 'mate' over and over in her head. It was the only thing Marley could think of. She narrowed her eyes on the soft flesh of Zara's shoulder when she pulled her up from the floor.

She pushed Zara down on the bed on her stomach. With a groan, she followed her and knelt at Zara's feet. She slowly ran her hand along Zara's body, watching goosebumps appear. The smell of her soon-to-be mate was overwhelming. Her tangy arousal was waiting on Marley.

Her fangs had dropped down, her animal refusing to settle until they'd had the taste of Zara's blood in their mouth. Once she bit Zara's flesh and marked her, her saliva would send an enzyme into

Zara's system, and her body's aging process would be altered. She would be able to live a long, fulfilling life with Marley.

Marley moved to cover Zara's body with hers. They both let out breathless moans. She trailed open-mouth kisses along Zara's shoulders, brushing her blonde hair out the way. She reached around and gripped Zara's breasts in her hands as she continued to slowly rub herself against Zara.

"Marley," Zara gasped, digging her nails into the comforter.

Zara spread her legs open while Marley rubbed her breasts along Zara's back. The feel of Zara's bottom sliding against her pussy was heavenly. She gripped Zara tight. She scraped her fangs along her shoulder muscles, teasing Zara.

She pinched Zara's nipples hard while thrusting her hips in rhythm with Zara. She slid down her lover's body, releasing her breasts to concentrate on tasting all of her. Her tongue blazed a trail down Zara's spine.

"Your scent, I can't get enough of it," Marley growled, licking the small of Zara's back before continuing her expedition south. Using her hands, she spread Zara's cheeks wide to allow her tongue to bathe Zara's forbidden hole.

"Oh." Zara released deep groan, arching her back, presenting more of her ass to Marley who took advantage of the new position.

Zara on her knees and elbows allowed Marley to dip her tongue down to Zara's slick core. She teased Zara's clit with her fingers while she thrust her tongue deep within Zara's folds. She trailed back up to Zara's puckered anus, coating it with her arousal. She let loose a growl at the taste of her mate on her tongue. She wanted more. She wished they were back home in California where she could break out one of the many toys she harbored. She pulled her finger that was coated with Zara's essence and slid it effortlessly into her tight entrance.

"Marley!"

She slowly turned her digit around and thrust it farther before bringing it almost all the way out. She inserted two, adjusting her body to where she could pummel Zara's anus with one hand while reaching around for her clit with her free hand. She may not have her toys with her, but she would make do without them.

Zara's body trembled while Marley continued to assault her with both hands. She loved being able to have her hands full of her mate. Zara rocked her body, setting a rhythm while taking Marley's invasion.

"Wait until we get home, my love. I have just the thing to go right here," she murmured, sliding her fingers out to gather more of Zara's juices to her anus before thrusting her fingers back in. "I promise you'll love it."

"I love what you're doing to me now," Zara gasped, her body shaking with each thrust of her hips.

Marley wasn't ready for Zara to reach her orgasm yet. She wanted to draw out their mating. It had to be just perfect.

"There's more, honey," she promised, pulling back from Zara and pushing her down on the bed.

Her chest rumbled with a deep growl. She flipped Zara onto her back and immediately thrust her legs apart. Zara's gaze met hers. She smiled a devilish grin as she positioned Zara's legs up and wide. She leaned forward and brushed her aching clit across Zara's.

"God, yes!" Zara shouted, gripping Marley's hips. She tossed her leg over Zara's, putting them in a perfect scissoring position.

"You're pussy is so wet," she muttered, loving the

sensation of their two clits sliding effortlessly across each other.

"Yours is, too," Zara gasped. "Faster. I'm almost there."

Marley reached down and gripped one of Zara's breast in her hands while she rode her harder. Both of their hips moved in harmony with each other. Their cries and moans filled the air.

Their movements quickened.

Marley leaned over Zara who immediately latched on to her breast, sucking it deep into her hot mouth. Marley threw her head back in ecstasy.

"Yes!" Marley cried out, quickly losing control of herself. Her body shook from the emotions coursing through her. Her hips were moving on autopilot when her orgasm slammed into her. She released a bellowing cry while the waves of her orgasm washed over her.

Zara let go of Marley's breast as she let loose a scream. Marley roared, leaning forward and clamped down on Zara's shoulder, piercing her soft flesh with her fangs.

Her wolf howled.

Her mouth filled with the copper substance of Zara. She swallowed, enjoying the true taste of her.

She pulled back, her body falling completely onto Zara.

Her gaze flew to Zara, finding them closed and a single tear disappearing into her hairline.

"Did I hurt you?" she gasped, trying to get ahold of her animal and her breath. She repositioned her body, resting in the valley of Zara's thighs.

Zara opened her eyes and shook her head, meeting Marley's. A wide smile spread across her face. She reached up and brushed the tear from Zara's face.

"No."

"Then why the tears?"

"It's tears of joy, mate," Zara whispered with a chuckle.

Relief filled Marley at the thought she hadn't hurt Zara. Marley's heart melted at hearing the endearment coming from Zara's lips.

"I love you, mate," Marley murmured.

She lowered her head and began licking Zara's wound. It would be healed by morning and would leave a permanent mark every shifter would identify as Marley's mate. The animal in her knew they had caused slight pain in their mate, and now they had to ensure the wound healed properly. The enzymes in Marley's saliva would help.

It was all part of being the mate of a wolf shifter. The dominant one would always care for the submissive in the relationship.

Marley and her wolf would cherish Zara for all eternity. She would be the soul focus of Marley's life.

Pleasing Zara would be Marley's life mission.

———

"What is it?" Zara whispered, propping herself up on her elbow. She had awakened from her light sleep to the feel of Marley moving to sit on the edge of the bed.

"I don't know. I heard something out there." Marley pointed to the window. She stood and walked over to it. The moonlight showcased her naked frame. She stood there for a few seconds before stalking to the door.

"Where are you going?"

"I'm going to look around. My wolf won't settle down until I check it out."

"I'll come with you." Zara sat up.

"No, I'll be quick. It's probably nothing but an animal."

Marley waved, but Zara was having none of it. Marley disappeared from the room. Zara shook her head at her stubborn mate. She'd be damned if Marley went outside in the unknown alone. Zara may not be a wolf shifter, but she could help in some way if something jumped off.

Zara scrambled from the bed and threw on a t-shirt and her bikini bottoms. She rushed from the room and made her way down the dark hallway. Not seeing Marley in any part of the house, she released a curse. Zara walked through the kitchen and found the patio door ajar. She slid it open and stepped out onto the patio.

There was no sign of Marley.

"Geesh, she's fast," Zara muttered.

She walked down the stairs and wasn't sure which way to go. Thankfully, the moon was high, providing some light. A gentle breeze blew past, sending a chill through Zara's body. Her gut clenched, but she continued on and marched around the house.

Alarms in the back of her mind were screaming for her to go back.

There was no way she would let Marley be out here without help. Voices floated through the air as she got closer to the front of the house. She moved near the building and peeked around the corner and held back a gasp.

Marley stood facing two other figures. A man with long, dark hair and a woman with light-colored hair. From where she stood, they both appeared to be very pale. She swallowed and remained still, straining to hear the conversation.

Her heart slammed against her chest hearing the man's words.

"Give us the human."

CHAPTER FIFTEEN

"Not a chance in hell," Marley growled, standing firm in her answer. She meant it. There was no way she would give Zara over to the bloodthirsty vampires standing before her.

"I can practically smell her on you. You've mated with her. The aroma of her blood is still on you," the female taunted.

"Wren, she acts like we can't just take the human for us. She would make a delicious meal as a welcoming gift. Looks as if they made themselves very comfortable in our vacation home," the male said. He flashed his fangs, the moonlight showcasing them.

Marley's gums stretched and burned as her own

descended. Her muscles grew tense while she narrowed her eyes on the two. She just prayed Zara had stayed in the house.

"Nostro, we could have such fun with both of them. Imagine a wolf shifter. Her blood will be powerful and sweet," Wren suggested.

"No one will be feeding on anyone," Marley snapped. Her animal was close to the surface. She fought the change, praying she didn't have to fight two vampires. This was the night of her mating, she should be in the bed with her mate enjoying what was between her thighs. "We will leave. We were having issues with our boat and found this island. I'll even pay you for the use of your home."

"You think we want your money?" Nostro barked a laugh. "No, give us the human, and we will let you leave. Alive."

"Never," Marley growled, her animal bursting forth. Marley stood on all fours with a deep growling, warning the two vampires away.

"As if we're supposed to be afraid of a wolf." Wren flashed her fangs and took a step forward.

"Look what we have here. The human followed you." Nostro pointed to a place over her shoulder.

The wind blew, and this time Marley picked up Zara's scent.

Shit.

Marley moved her body to put herself in the direct path of the vampires and Zara.

"Look at her, protecting her mate." Wren pouted. "Too bad we'll kill her before she can see us bleed her little bitch dry."

Wren sped forward toward Zara, but Marley was able to catch the female vampire. A scream echoed in the air that could only be Zara's. Wren's body slammed into Marley's, but Marley was able to maintain her footing. Her wolf growled as she snapped her fangs.

She hoped like hell Zara ran back into the house.

Nostro rushed past them and took off toward the back yard.

Marley lunged at Wren and latched on to the vampire's arm. She let loose a scream and threw her arm out, sending Marley flying through the air.

Wren took off running toward the backyard. Marley righted her footing and sped off behind the vampire, close on her heels. She leaped through the air and landed on the female vampire with a fierce growl.

The vampire flipped over and tried to throw Marley off her, but Marley dug her claws into the vampire's chest, pinning her to the ground.

"Get off me, wolf," the vampire screeched but was unable to fight Marley off. Her alpha wolf was overpowering the vampire.

Her wolf was in a frenzy to protect her mate. There was no way this vampire was going to ever put her hands on Zara. Her wolf snapped her jaws at Wren, whose feeble attempt to ward Marley off was fairly useless.

Marley's wolf sank her fangs into the vampire's neck, muffling her scream. The wolf had death for the vampire on her mind. Her fangs tore through the flesh of Wren, silencing her forever. Marley spit out the sour-tasting skin, watching Wren's body flail on the ground. Her blood rushed out of her body, spilling onto the dirt beneath her. Wren's eyes were now fixed as her life force left her.

Marley's wolf stood on top of the vampire and threw her head back and released a deep howl.

A cry went through the air, snagging Marley's attention. Her gaze turned and found Nostro dragging Zara in front of him. His gaze flickered to his dead companion while Marley stepped forward with her attention locked on the male vampire who had his hands on her mate.

"You've killed my mate," Nostro snapped. His bloodthirsty eyes moved to Marley.

Her wolf gave a warning growl as she slowly stepped toward him.

"Marley," Zara whimpered.

The vampire held her by the throat with one hand. His now crimson eyes didn't budge from Marley's fierce glare.

"It would be so easy for me to kill yours," he threatened. "All it would take would be a simple snap of her neck, or how about I sink my fangs in arteries and drain her before you?"

Marley responded with a more profound growl in response to his words. He wouldn't reach the beach before Marley's wolf would be pouncing on him.

"Do you know who she is?" Zara whispered. Fear was prevalent in her eyes, but her voice was steady and strong.

"She's a wolf—"

"Oh, no. She's not just any wolf. She's the daughter of Evan Gerwulf, and if you kill either me or her, you will pay dearly for it."

Uncertainty flashed in his eyes as he paused. "Gerwulf, as in the alpha of The Nightstar Pack?"

"Yes." Zara nodded, her eyes pleading to be let go.

Nostro's eyes narrowed on Marley, the uncertainty disappearing.

"Well, I didn't have beef with the alpha before, but seeing how his daughter killed my mate, I will just have to return the favor." Nostro bared his fangs while Zara whimpered as he tightened his grip on her throat.

Marley's wolf took off toward them with her fangs bared. Nostro tossed Zara to the side right when Marley's wolf slammed into him.

———

Zara had never been so scared in her life. She watched Marley fight the large male vampire. Zara gripped her neck in an attempt to soothe her aching throat. The vampire's grip had dug into her skin, cutting her air off. She knew the paranormal world was dangerous but had never been thrown into the middle of it. She crawled to a safe distance, willing Marley to win.

She had to.

If the vampire won, there was no telling what he'd do with her.

Growls filled the air as Marley circled the

vampire. She leaped forward, going for his throat. He tossed her aside as if she wasn't a massive animal. She didn't stay down long. Within seconds she was rolling over and on the attack again.

Zara's gaze flew around the yard, looking for anything she could use to aid in the fight. She may be a human, but she was determined to ensure her mate survived. They had just taken the step to spend all eternity together, and Zara would be damned if it would be snatched away from her.

She scrambled to her feet and took off toward a bunch of foliage that was on the ground. She searched for a weapon she could make. The old tale of staking a vampire through the heart was real.

A pain-filled howl ripped through the air. Zara's gaze landed on Marley's body falling to the earth.

A perfect tree branch lay on the ground as if a gift from the heavens.

She snatched it up and ran with it in her hands. She released a scream as the vampire turned to her. The edge of the branch pierced his chest.

Shock resonated on his face while she held the branch tight in her hand. Dark fluid ran out of his chest around the makeshift stake.

"What—" His word was garbled.

With another scream, she pushed the stake even farther when his knees gave out. His already pale face grew ash gray. His eyes were wide in disbelief.

Zara was sure he didn't see his life coming to an end at the hands of a puny human.

"Die!" she screamed in his face with one more good shove of the branch.

His body fell over onto the ground, deathly still.

Her breaths were coming fast while she stood over his body. It was motionless, and she searched for any signs of life. Movement from the corner of her eyes caught her attention. She turned and found Marley's wolf lying on the ground, writhing around in pain.

"Marley!" she shouted, running to her mate.

Marley's wolf whined when she tried to stand. Zara caught the sight of blood dripping from her stomach. The sun, finally deciding to rise, slowly brought more light for Zara to try to see what was bleeding on Marley.

"Stay down. Let me take a look." Zara pushed Marley back down.

Marley gave a loud snort and nodded toward the vampires.

Zara turned, and her gaze was met with two steaming vampire bodies. The sun's rays were causing the disintegration of the corpses. Zara had never seen what sunlight could truly do to vampires. She had always thought it to be a rumor, but as she watched, the sun rose higher. The vampire's bodies combusted into flames.

Zara shifted her body to where Marley could rest her head on her lap as they watched the bodies burn. The flames grew, licking the air as if trying to reach the sky. Soon the bodies turned to ash, and the fire slowly burned out, leaving two white piles of dust.

Zara ran her fingers through Marley's fur to settle the wolf down. Small growls vibrated deep in the wolf's chest.

"Calm down. It's over," Zara whispered, praying it truly was. "I need to speak to Marley. Can you let her out, please?"

Marley's wolf snorted, her pain-filled eyes glancing at her. She pulled away and stood, walking a few steps away. Zara watched the change overcome her, and a minute later a naked Marley fell to the ground with a grunt.

"Marley!" Zara rushed toward her mate, concern filling her chest. "What happened?"

"The vampire had a silver knife in his hand." Marley turned over with Zara's help.

Zara placed her mate's head in her lap again and brushed her hair from her face.

"What do you need me to do?" Zara whispered.

"If there ever is a fight between me and a vampire, next time you run."

CHAPTER SIXTEEN

Zara helped a weak Marley into the living room, guiding her to the couch.

"Shouldn't you shift or something?" she asked. She was sure if Marley shifted again, it would help push the silver from her system and help heal her wound.

"I will, but now we need to call for help. We don't know if there are any other vampires out there. If there are, I'm in no shape to fight them."

Marley released a hiss as she eased down on the couch. Zara's heart raced at the sight of her pale face. She'd never seen Marley like this before and she was trying to calm her nerves.

"Let me at least get you something to press on

the wound," Zara gushed, turning on her heel and heading down the hall.

"Grab the satellite phone off the nightstand in the room," Marley weakly called out.

Zara opened the hallway closet and found some towels. She grabbed a few and rushed into their bedroom. The yellow phone was sitting where Marley said it would be. She snatched it up and ran back into the living room, not wanting to leave Marley alone for too long.

She arrived to find Marley looking paler by the minute. Her hands were coated with her blood as she tried to stop the flow.

"Here." Zara moved to kneel beside the couch and lifted Marley's hand out of the way. The wound was rugged and red with a slow stream of crimson fluid. She pressed the towel to the injury in hopes to stop the blood flow. Her heart pounded at the grimace that crossed Marley's face.

"Turn the phone on. I'll give you the number to my father's cell phone." Marley motioned for the phone.

Zara snatched it with her free hand and pressed the ON button. The screen lit up, displaying the time and date.

"How will they know where we are?"

"Most satellite phones are built with location tracking. They will be able to find us. Once my father gets his helicopter in the air, there's no telling how long until he gets here."

Zara nodded, dialing the numbers Marley rattled off. Her hand shook as she put it on speakerphone. It rung once before the alpha's growl filled the air.

"Who is this?"

Zara's eyes widened, and she held the phone closer to Marley.

"Daddy?" Marley bit her lip as if to hold back a sob.

Zara had to admit the sound of the pissed-off alpha was music to her ears as well.

"Marley?" The tone of his voice immediately changed to one of a concerned father.

"Yes, it's me and Zara." Marley nodded as if her father would be able to see her.

"Thank the heavens. Where are you?" he asked, relief flooding his voice.

"We don't know. We found an island with a small house on it, and it had a satellite phone," Zara replied.

Their eyes locked, and Zara knew not to mention the vampires at this time.

"I'm tracking you know." His voice grew muffled

as he snapped orders to someone. "What happened to you two? We've been searching for weeks for you."

"We ran into a bad storm that knocked everything off in the boat. We were floating aimlessly in the ocean and finally found the private island," Marley summed it up. She grimaced, holding the towel closer to her.

"Are you injured?" The wolf in him must have picked up Marley's discomforted.

"Nothing that won't heal with a shift or two," Marley murmured.

"What happened?" he demanded.

Zara swallowed hard at the harsh tone of his voice. She knew it wasn't directed at Marley. The alpha was very protective of his only daughter, and if the vampire wasn't already dead, he would be.

"Let's just say I was protecting my mate." Marley's lips curved into a small smile as she reached for Zara's hand with one of hers.

Zara took it and squeezed, knowing she would be forever grateful to have lived through this ordeal. They would have the rest of their lives to be together.

"You finally told Zara?"

"Yeah, Daddy. This time we've spent together made us realize just how much we are meant to be together."

Zara's heart jumped at Marley's words. She leaned forward and pressed a small kiss to Marley's lips.

I love you, she mouthed to her mate.

"We are locked on your location. We should be there in about four to six hours. Shift and heal. Get some rest. We'll be there soon."

Marley had never thought she would be so happy to hear the sounds of helicopter blades whipping through the air. They had gathered their belongings to wait out the arrival of her father.

"Do you think this was the vampires' home?" Zara asked from her perch beside Marley.

They had come outside to await the arrival of their rescue team.

"No. The house wasn't built for vampires. It has too many windows. I'm sure who ever owned this place is long dead if the vampires were claiming this place." Marley stood from her spot on the stairs. She grimaced at the slight ache in her abdomen.

"Do you need to shift again?" Zara asked, coming to stand by her side. Worry was etched on her face.

Marley leaned over and pressed her forehead

against Zara's. "I'll be fine. The major injury is gone, but the ache will be there for another day or so. It's not so bad," she declared, but Zara didn't seem convinced.

"That's not what your face showed." Zara cocked her eyebrow but wrapped her arm around Marley's waist.

The wolf in Marley wouldn't want their mate to worry about them. Her and the beast were too stubborn and would want their mate to know they would always be strong enough to protect her.

"I'm sure. Once we get home, I'll be fine," Marley promised.

Zara's eyes showed her disbelief, but she nodded. They grabbed their bags and began to make the trek to the beach where the helicopter had flown to.

Marley paused and turned to stare at the house. She wondered what had happened to the original owners. This home would be a forever part of her and Zara's life.

It was the place where they'd mated.

"What is it?" Zara's voice broke through her thoughts.

Marley turned her attention to Zara's face and smiled. She tipped her mate's chin up and pressed a soft kiss to Zara's lips.

"I just wanted to have one more look at the place where you became my mate," she admitted.

Zara's face softened, her body melting against Marley's.

"Well, I already have a plot or two for a story. Two lovers on a secluded island...it's going to be amazing," Zara bragged. She reached up and ran her finger along Marley's bottom lip.

Marley smiled, knowing with Zara's imagination, the book would fly off the shelves. Her readers loved her so much.

"Lets get home and we can create new memories," Zara suggested, her voice growing husky.

"Oh, I'm going to hold you to this," Marley growled.

They both broke out into giggles, turning and walking down the sandy path.

Voices could be heard off in the distance, urging Marley forward. She stepped in front of Zara, wanting to ensure it was her father and his men. She didn't want to take the chance it could be someone else.

They drew closer to the beach, and the sound of the waves crashing along the shore filled the air. A distinctive voice barked orders, and Marley's heart raced. She turned and grabbed Zara's hand, pulling her behind her.

They broke through the brush and found a black helicopter parked on the beach with *Gerwulf Enterprises* splashed along the side. The massive dark bird was out of place on the private island, but it was one of the best things Marley had seen. A few men stood outside the copter, but it was only one who captured Marley's attention.

Marley's eyes met the familiar, tense ones of her father, and she lost it. Her brother, Conon, stood beside him with an identical expression.

"Father!" she choked out his name, too full of emotions.

The tortured look on his face was enough to send tears flowing down hers. She released Zara's hand and took off running toward his open arms. Her body slammed into his, with his strong arms wrapping themselves around her in a crushing hug.

"Marley, you girls have aged me at least ten years," her father muttered.

A hiccupped laugh escaped Marley's lips as she squeezed her father tight. She stepped back and took in Conon. Her elder brother, the future alpha of their pack, was almost an identical copy of their father. His lips broke into a wide grin.

"It's good to have you back, sis." Conon's voice was gruff while he opened his arms.

She moved into her big brother's embrace and squeezed him hard.

"I can't believe I'm saying this, but I did miss you," she murmured.

The two of them had always had a fierce sibling rivalry, but when it came down to family, there was nothing either of them wouldn't do for the other. She pulled back and looked around for Zara. Her mate was standing back as if to give them privacy. Marley motioned for Zara to come closer.

Zara walked up and took Marley's offered hand.

"It's good to see you again, Alpha. Conon." Zara smiled, leaning against Marley.

"You, too."

The alpha's and Conon's gazes dropped to Zara's shoulder, taking in her mating mark. Marley's wolf stood up taller, proud her mate had accepted her.

"Welcome to the family."

Marley's heart swelled watching her father offer his hand to Zara. He pulled her in a tight embrace, showing acceptance of her mate. Her brother rested his arm around her shoulders.

"It's about time, sis." He pressed a kiss to her forehead.

A wide smile spread across her face.

CHAPTER SEVENTEEN

"Mom, I promise, I'm fine." Zara sighed.

Once they had reached the mainland, they had been taken to the local hospital to be checked out. From what Zara had heard, Marley had immediately been given a clean bill of health. Her shifter genes protected her. Even with the injury she'd got from the fight with the vampires, she had been released immediately.

For Zara, being human, the doctors had drawn tons of blood to ensure she was healthy. Physically she felt fine, but mentally she was drained.

Between her overprotective parents and dodging the media, she was tired.

"I just kept praying they would find you girls safe

and sound," April York whispered. She pushed Zara's hair back from her face.

Zara's heart tugged at the unshed tears sitting on her mother's eyelids.

"I was with Marley, Mom. You know she wouldn't let anything happen to me. She's a shifter," she murmured.

Her father sat on the other side of the hospital bed and gripped her hand.

They were waiting for the physician to come back with the results of the testing he had run. Hopefully, she wouldn't have to be admitted. Zara just wanted to go home and take the longest hot shower known to man.

"That is the only thing that offered me some comfort. You girls have always been thick as thieves, and I'm sure her wolf would protect you," John York said.

Zara smiled at her father and squeezed his hand. There was no way she'd tell them about the vampire attack. Her parents had already been through hell thinking they had lost their only child.

The sound of a phone ringing cut through the air, breaking the silence. Zara's pulse paused in her throat from the shrill jangle. A nervous giggle escaped her as she settled back against the plush pillows.

April stood and grabbed the phone. "Hello?" She rolled her eyes. "As I said before, no comment." She slammed the receiver down in the cradle and ran her hand through her dark-blonde hair.

"Media again?" John asked.

"Yes, they are like vultures. We've just got our daughter back, and they will not take no for an answer."

Zara swallowed hard. Since returning, she'd heard how her and Marley had been all over the news. The disappearance of a billionaire alpha's daughter was the top story, and with her reappearance, everyone wanted a piece of the tale.

"I'm sure I'll be long forgotten after a while," Zara offered.

"I'm almost tempted to disconnect our home number for now. Ever since the story broke that you two were missing, our phones have been ringing off the hook with reporters. Just knowing there was a chance you'd call the house—" Her father's voice cracked. His eyes filled with tears as he stared at her.

"Oh, Daddy. I'm here. I'm safe," she cried out, throwing her arms around his neck and crushing him to her. She'd never seen John York get so emotional before, and it practically tore her heart from her chest.

He sniffled and cleared his throat while holding her tight in his arms.

"We didn't know what we would have done if you hadn't returned to us." Her mother sniffed, sitting back on the edge of the bed.

Zara pulled back from her father and offered reassuring smiles. They were interrupted by a knock at the door.

"Should I come back?" The physician was standing at the door with his clipboard in his hands.

"Nonsense, please come in." John stood and waved the doctor and his associates into the room.

Zara sent up a little prayer that everything was fine and she'd be able to go home. She hadn't had a chance to see or speak to Marley since they'd whisked her away. She needed to see her mate. Her heart longed to see Marley's bright smile.

"Well, I have great news," Dr. Smyth announced.

Zara sat up with his words. Her heart raced with the anticipation of leaving the hospital.

"That's great. How's our daughter's bloodwork?" April asked, gripping Zara's hand.

Zara held back a wince from strength of her mother's grip.

"Everything checked out. She's just a little malnourished, but it will be corrected now she's home and can get good meals."

A sigh went around the room.

"Thank you, Doctor." Zara smiled at Dr. Smyth. "The news is almost as good as hearing I was being rescued."

Everyone chuckled. Even her parents. She sighed and was ready to break out of the hospital. She had a mate to get to. She was sure Marley was worrying over her.

"Your nurse will be in soon to discharge you. Just promise to get some rest, drink plenty of water, and have a burger or two." Dr. Smyth laughed, stepping over to her.

His residents chuckled by his side.

"That I can promise you." Zara snorted, shaking the doctor's hand. She couldn't wait to pig out on the largest bacon cheeseburger she could get her hands on.

"Thank you, Dr. Smyth." Her parents both stood and shook the doctor's hand.

"My pleasure. Any issues, come back, but I think she just needs rest."

Zara waved to the doctor and watched him and his team leave the room.

"I'm so ready to go home and take a hot shower," Zara grumbled, tossing her legs over the side of the bed. Since she'd arrived, her clothes had been taken and properly discarded in the trash. She looked down at the borrowed hospital pants and gown.

The floral print just doesn't do anything for me. She giggled.

"Why don't you come home with us for a few days?" her mother asked, concern etched on her face.

Both of her parents stared at her while waiting for an answer.

Seeing her hesitation, her mother rushed to sit on the side of the bed. "I'll cook and bake anything you want. Just let us spoil and love on you a few days before you go back to your place."

Her mother was a dirty fighter. She knew Zara wouldn't be able to resist her cooking. April York had a way around the kitchen that would make the strictest dieter forget their diet.

"Just a few days," her father murmured.

How could she refuse such plea from the people who'd birthed her?

"Okay. A few days," she agreed.

Her mother's squeal filled the air as she wrapped Zara up in a firm hug.

"Let's get you out of here," her mother gushed.

Her nurse entered the room and gave Zara her discharge papers. Per hospital policy, Zara had to ride in a wheelchair, and her mother refused to let her be a rebel and walk out of the building.

"Do you know where Marley is?" she asked.

Her mother pushed her through the hallways of the hospital.

"I believe her and her family are in the waiting room," her father replied.

She turned to look at him at the tone in his voice. He refused to meet her eyes, and a small alarm went off in the back of her mind.

"What's wrong?" she asked.

"Don't worry about it." Her father shook his head. His body grew tense once they passed through the doors to the waiting area.

Marley sat in the corner next to her parents. Her face brightened when Zara was wheeled in.

"Zara!" Marley jumped from her chair and rushed across the room. She threw her arms around Zara in a tight hug.

"I'm okay, Marley." Zara chuckled, squeezing her tight.

Marley pulled back, her gaze frantically looking Zara over as if to check her out herself.

Zara reached for her hand and entwined their fingers. "Really, I am. Doctor said I was just a little dehydrated and malnourished. He ordered me to eat a burger or two and rest."

"We are going to take our daughter home now." The tone in her father's voice again meant Zara whipped her head around. His lips were pressed together in a firm line. Where was this coming from? He had just told her he'd felt comforted by Marley being with her. "She's has a rough time and needs to be around just family."

She widened her eyes at him, unable to believe how he was acting.

"But she's fine," Evan replied in a soft tone.

His hard eyes met her father's, and she swallowed hard at the silent standoff between the two.

"If she weren't, the physicians would keep her."

"Don't worry about my daughter. You tend to yours and I'll take care of mine."

"Daddy, seriously, I'm fine—"

"I saw the wound on your shoulder. It looks like an animal tore into you," her father snapped, cutting her off.

Zara jumped, not realizing when she had

changed her clothes he'd seen her mating bite. She had wanted to tell her parents once they were home and settled.

"No one wants to talk about why my daughter came home mangled."

The other shifters that were with Evan and Marley moved to stand behind the alpha.

"What are you trying to say?" Evan's face darkened, his attention focused on her father.

Zara glanced at Marley, unsure what to do. Marley stood by her father, shocked. Her mouth moved, but no words came out.

"John, you know my daughter took care of Zara."

"I don't know what really happened out there. All I know is my daughter was lost out in God knows where—"

"John, let's go, honey. You're making a scene," her mother spoke up from behind Zara.

Zara glanced around the waiting area, and all eyes were on them.

"Look, we'll come by the house and talk about this—"

"No. You people have done enough." Her father raised his hand, cutting the alpha off.

Zara's mouth dropped in shock. She couldn't believe her father. A growl ripped through the air.

Evan didn't take too kind to being cut off and dismissed.

"Dad, no," Marley gasped, jumping in front of the alpha.

His murderous eyes were locked on John who turned his back on them. Zara, unable to speak, stared at her father as if he had grown a second head.

Who is this man?

"We're done here. Let's get Zara home, April." John waved to her mother.

Marley's tear-filled eyes met hers as her mother wheeled her past them.

I'll call you, she mouthed to Marley.

Zara sat in her chair, hands folded, unsure what had just happened. When they got home and her father calmed down, they would have to have a long talk.

CHAPTER EIGHTEEN

"It's going to be okay, Marley," her father said, following behind her into her cabin.

She looked around, and the living room was just as she had left it. She was glad to be home, but it was all dimmed now by the way the Yorks had acted at the hospital. She should have been bringing her mate home, but that dream had been quickly shattered.

She should have known something was off when the Yorks refused to allow anyone to come back to see Zara in the hospital. She had blamed it on them being so frantic when they had first arrived back at the mainland.

"Why was Mr. York acting like I did something to Zara? I would never harm her!" She spun around with tears trailing down her face. Her heart had broken watching the Yorks wheel Zara away from her. Her wolf wanted to break free and follow them.

"They are human," he began, shutting the door behind him and moving to her.

She flew into her father's arms. She should be strong, but one look at her father, and she just melted. Her wolf couldn't bear to be away from their mate. They had completed the mating bond.

"Zara belongs here with me." She sniffed.

"And she will come to you." He gently wiped the tears from her face. "You need to be strong, Marley Gerwulf. Mating a human is not going to be easy. Some people still have problems with shifters. We've known the Yorks for a long time, and they will come around. I'm sure they are just in protective mode right now. They almost lost their only daughter. I know what they had been experiencing."

Marley studied her father's eyes, and a haunted look passed through them. She bit her lip and nodded. She knew what her and Zara had gone through but couldn't imagine if the shoe was on the other foot. She would go crazy if something happened to one of her parents or her brother.

"What should I do?" she asked, pulling away from her father. She walked over to her couch and dropped down onto it.

"Give them time. I'm sure Zara will speak with them. John just wasn't in his right mind." He came and sat next to her. "I let my emotions cloud my best judgment. I came close to attacking a human."

She sighed and glanced at her father. It had been one of the first times she'd seen him lose his cool at a human. At a fellow shifter, of course. As the alpha, over the years he had been challenged and fought and defeated other wolves who'd thought they were strong enough to take his place. The life of a shifter involved violence. A human against a shifter would be an unfair fight. Zara's father wouldn't have stood a chance against Evan.

"It's okay, Daddy. You were protecting me. He blames me for what happened on the boat. I could see it in his eyes." She sniffed again, tucking her feet beneath her.

"Spontaneous storms are not your fault," her father snapped. He ran a hand through his hair and patted her on her knee. "I'm sure you did everything how you were taught. Because of that, both of you girls were able to survive and get home. They'll come around."

"And if they don't?" Her wolf paced inside with a grumble. She grew impatient and want to run off and bring Zara home.

"They will. Zara loves you. I can see it in her eyes. She always has and just didn't realize it. You two will be together."

She smiled and reached for her father's hand. He squeezed it and gave her a lopsided smile. It felt good to be home and be able to talk to her father. He was the best counselor and was so wise. She trusted in what he advised.

"So now what?"

"Now we go for a pack run. The pack has been antsy waiting for your return. They want to see you. Up for it?" He stood and held out his hand to her.

She glanced at it, and her wolf gave a yip as if to answer her alpha.

"Of course." She took his hand and allowed him to pull her up from the couch. "I need to go for a run. Maybe it will help settle my wolf." She followed him toward the door.

"I doubt she settles down until your mate is here with you," he threw over his shoulder.

She sighed and shook her head. He was right. Her wolf would be content once Zara was in her arms again.

"What happened on that island?" he asked.

She froze and stared at him. He turned, probably sensing her hesitation, and cocked and eyebrow at her. She swallowed, hoping they would avoid this particular conversation. She'd handled it, and they'd made it through.

"What are you talking about?" She tried to act like she didn't know what he was referring to.

He crossed his arms in front of his massive chest. His eyes narrowed on her, and she suddenly felt like she was a nine-year-old pup about to get scolded by her father. She rolled her eyes and sighed.

"We ran into a tiny bit of vampire trouble. Turned out the island was a little getaway for two vampires. They thought they would be able to take my mate from me. They were mistaken. They paid for their mistake with their lives." Her voice ended on a growl, her animal coming to the surface. If she could, she'd kill the two vampires again for even glancing at Zara.

A proud look appeared on her father's face. Protecting one's mate was vital. There was no way that she would have let those vampires get their hands on Zara. Apparently satisfied, he gave a nod before turning and opening the front door. He had raised his children to be able to fight and take care of themselves.

They walked out onto her porch and stripped their clothes off. She jogged down the stairs and called for her animal. Her dark fur burst forth, covering her naked flesh while her gums burned from her canines descending. She fell to the ground, her body contorting and shifting.

Her wolf stood proud and pawed at the ground. Her beast let loose a lovesick whine, wanting to see Zara. Her wolf loved when her mate ran her fingers through her fur.

She spun and found her father in his animal form by her side. He tossed his head and strolled away toward the woods. She followed behind him, praying that everything would be as he'd said.

***

Zara toweled off, drying her body. She was in her old room at her parents' house. The shower she'd taken had been hot and helped relax her aching muscles. Now that she'd had time to think about her father's outburst at the hospital, she grew angry.

She'd been friends with Marley since she'd been sixteen. Their families knew each other. Never in all the years had her parents treated Marley different for being a shifter. They'd treated her like another daughter.

Zara strode over to her bed and grabbed her

clothes. She'd always had some stashed at her parents', and her soft yoga pants and t-shirt were perfect. Hopping around on one foot, she thrust her legs in her pants before walking over to her dresser in search of undergarments.

"Guess I will have to go commando," she muttered, opening the drawers of her dresser. She could have sworn she'd left some here but didn't see anything but random t-shirts and shorts. Her shoulders slumped as a sigh slipped from her lips. There weren't any bras.

She took herself in, glancing at the mirror on her dresser. She had a deep tan, and her hair even seemed lighter, but what she focused on was the mark on her shoulder. Her core clenched thinking of the night that Marley had marked her. A wistful smile played on her lips as the memories of their mating came to mind. She reached up and slowly ran her fingers over the beautiful scar.

They belonged together.

She'd make her parents see. If they didn't accept what she was about to tell them, then they'd leave her no choice but to choose between the love of her life and them.

She'd choose Marley.

Throwing her shirt over head, she quickly

combed through her hair and found a pair of sandals tucked underneath her bed. She left her room, determined to talk to her parents and find out what the hell was going on with them.

Jogging down the stairs, she heard voices coming from the living room. She made her way to it and paused in the doorway.

Her father sat in his recliner with a drink in his hand. He looked as if he'd aged ten years. Her mother turned, wiping tears from her cheeks. She tried to smile, but there was no faking it.

Something was wrong.

"Zara, honey. How was your shower?" her mother asked, standing from the couch.

Zara stepped into the living room and wiped her hands on her pants. Her father took a healthy sip of his drink and watched her.

"We need to talk," she announced. She beat down her nerves, and her confidence slowly increased. She thought of what her and Marley had been through. Marley had fought vampires to save her. She could deal with her parents.

CHAPTER NINETEEN

"**B**ut of course, dear. You can talk to us about anything." Her father motioned to the couch, but she shook her head.

She'd rather stand for this discussion.

"Is something wrong?" Worry was written all over her mother's face. Her eyes were full of concern while she came over to Zara. She rubbed Zara's back, bringing a small smile to her lips.

"No, nothing is wrong. It's so good to be home. We need to talk about what I went through out there."

"Come, baby. Sit down. We do want to hear what happened." Her mother ushered her to the couch, and she took a seat.

Zara noticed her hands shaking, and she clamped them together on her lap.

"I can do this," she muttered to herself.

"If you feel you are ready," her father began.

"I am." She cleared her throat and glanced between her parents and knew she needed to be upfront with them.

"The trip began great. Sun, ocean, and just having fun sailing. I was getting writing done and working on my tan. It started as the best vacation I could have. Thoughts of Bo didn't even cross my mind."

"As it shouldn't," her father mumbled, taking another sip of his drink. He'd never been a fan of Bo, and after the news broke that he'd cheated on Zara, her ex had climbed to the top of her father's shit list.

"Then on the day the storm came, it had been beautiful. Clear-blue skies, the sun was high, and in a blink of an eye, clouds came and took it all away. There was no storm on the forecast, and when it came, it hit the boat hard." She paused, looking down at her hands, remembering how Marley had fought to keep their boat safe. She had been amazing.

"Oh my," her mother whispered. She reached out and took Zara's hand in hers.

Zara didn't object but instead squeezed her

mother's hand tight. Her heart settled feeling the support from her mother as she told her tale.

"Marley was awesome. She handled it like a seasoned veteran. I had laughed when she'd went over the boat and did a little service when we first arrived in Hawaii, but once the storm hit, I was so glad she did. If she wasn't as trained as she was, we probably wouldn't have made it."

She glanced up and met her father's eyes. Her heart skipped a beat from what she saw.

Fear.

He gripped his glass tight before knocking back the rest of it, breaking their stare. She swallowed hard and continued her story.

"You see, floating out in the middle of the ocean, with no one hearing our distress calls, made me realize how much life means. I took a hard look at my life and realized that I had been searching this entire time for the one person who would make me, and she'd been at my side this entire time."

"Well, of course Marley has been at your side. You two have been best friends since you were sixteen years old. Friendships like that don't just die." Her mother patted her hand with an innocent smile on her face.

"I don't think that's what she's talking about, my dear," her father murmured.

Zara focused her gaze to her father and found him staring out the window beside him. She turned her attention back to her mother who had frozen in place.

"Zara, what are you really saying?" her mother asked.

"I'm saying that I am Marley's mate. I always have been, but I just didn't know it."

Her mother's gasp filled the air. April studied Zara.

"But, Zara—"

"The mark on my shoulder wasn't from being attacked. This is Marley's mating mark. We've mated." Zara pulled her shirt to the side so her mother could see the marking up close. She was proud to show off that she belonged to Marley. No one would be able to take that from her. Not her parents, not the world.

Not anyone.

Her mother's gaze dropped to Zara's mating mark. She didn't say a word. The room remained quiet for what seemed an eternity.

"So you and Marley are...um...married in the way of the shifters?" Her mother's eyes grew wide.

Zara found her father's gaze on her. She could no longer read him.

"Yes, Mom. We love each other, and I want to spend the rest of my life with her." She smiled, a weight lifting from her shoulders with her announcement. She willed herself to remain strong. "All this time, she'd known that I was her mate. She did the honorable thing and didn't say anything. According to her, she wanted me in her life any way she could have me, even if it was just as a friend."

"And you are sure of this? How do you know this wasn't you being emotional and facing death?" her mother asked, concern filling her eyes.

"Because I knew in my heart that no matter what, Marley was the one for me. We belong together, and I'm telling you this because I want you to accept that I love Marley." She paused and glanced between her parents. Her heart would break if they couldn't accept that she and Marley were mated.

Her father cleared his throat, and her breath caught as she waited for his response. He had been extremely quiet since she'd stepped foot in the room. She never thought she would have to sit before her parents and ask for their blessing to be with someone.

"Daddy, say something," she whispered. She bit her lip to keep a sob from escaping her chest. No matter what, she was going to grab her things and go to Marley. She didn't want to be away from her any longer. Tears threatened to fall. She reached up and wiped them away, trying to clear her vision so she could see her father.

"Zara. I've known for a while that Marley felt more for you than friendship. It didn't take a rocket scientist to see the way she looked at you." He paused, running a hand across his face. He suddenly appeared tired and worn down. The stress of her being missing had taken its toll on him. "But I always wondered if today would come and how long would it take before you found out about her feelings."

"What are you saying, Daddy?" She was impatient and wanted him to get to the point.

John York was a man who could talk circles around anyone, and today was not the day that she needed the long-winded version of her father. She needed for him to get to the point.

He sat forward, resting his elbows on his knees. His eyes connected with hers, while her heart raced.

"I'm saying I'm worried about you, kiddo. If you two have truly mated in the eyes of the shifters, will her pack accept you? It's one thing that she's a wolf shifter and you're human, but you are both females. I don't want my baby girl hurt. I don't know what I would do if—"

"Oh, Daddy!" She pushed off the couch and rushed to him. She knelt on the floor before him and gripped his hands in hers. Tears slid down her cheeks, burning a warm trail along her skin. She smiled through her tears, meeting his concurred gaze. "Shifters are more accepting to same-sex couples than humans are. They believe in fate and that destiny decides who mates are. So see, Daddy, we were meant to be."

She blinked, clearing her vision to catch her father's nod. He brought their hands up to his lips, placing a kiss onto the back of hers.

"Ever since you've been missing, I was just so scared that I'd never see your beautiful smile again," he admitted.

"But I am here. Marley saved me and made sure we'd survived," she whispered.

Sniffles could be heard behind her. Zara glanced over her shoulder and found her mother smiling through her tears.

"I will be forever grateful to Marley, and if you love her and want to spend the rest of your life with her, then your momma and me will support you."

ARIEL MARIE

She jumped up and wrapped her arms around him in a firm hug. He stood from the chair and gathered her into his arms. Her sob broke through, and her body was wracked with tears. She felt another presence by her side and pulled back, finding her mother standing next to them. Her father opened his arms and tugged her mother close, too.

"Don't ever doubt our love for you, Zara York," her mother whispered, brushing her hair back away from her face.

A hiccup escaped Zara, and they all laughed, breaking the tension.

"We love you for you," her father said. "No matter what. You will always be our daughter. That will never change."

"I'm so sorry. This whole time I was scared that you wouldn't accept Marley, Dad. The way you acted at the hospital—"

"I was an ass." He cut her off with a shake of his head. "I had so many emotions swirling around in me that I don't know what came over me. I wanted to blame someone for what happened to you out on that ocean. Evan and Jena have always treated you like a daughter. I owe them an apology."

CHAPTER TWENTY

Marley's cheeks literally hurt from the fake smile she kept plastered to her face. Excitement was thick in the air while her people celebrated her return. A bonfire was lit, and the flames reached high in the sky. Usually she would be right in the middle of the festivities, but she couldn't take her mind off her mate. She sighed, glancing around at the hundreds of people who were gathered here tonight for her.

Her wolf paced, irritated that their mate wasn't there with them.

Soon, she murmured. She knew that deep in her heart Zara would come to her, but she was growing impatient.

"Stop being a bump on a log," her older brother said behind her.

She turned and glanced over her shoulder, finding Conon making his way to her.

She snorted, looking down at her seat—a log.

"Your jokes get worse the older you get, old man." She chuckled.

He sat next to her on the oversized log. She had been watching their people gather around the bonfire, having a great time. She couldn't make herself feel happy knowing she was currently separated from her mate. They should be here together.

"Stop looking so glum. Get up and go mingle. Everyone is here in your honor." Conon nudged her with his elbow.

He was trying to distract her, and if this was any other day, he would have succeeded, but her mind and her wolf were focused on her mate.

She shook her head and glanced around, taking in the crowd. Wolves in their human and animal form could be seen. She saw her parents speaking with a few members of the pack.

"It's hard to celebrate when I don't know what is going on with Zara and me," she admitted. She felt her brother's gaze on her and refused to turn to him. She was scared that if she did, her emotions would get the best of her, and she didn't want to seem weak in front of her brother.

"Look, sis. I've never told you this, but I thought you were crazy for never telling Zara. I don't know how you did it, but I have to say that you impressed the hell out of me. To go that long with your mate at your side and be unable to say anything or claim her, that took heart and was very unselfish."

Facing him, she saw the honesty in his face and was choked up with words. She nodded, smiling as he wrapped an arm around her and pulled her close to him in a tight hug.

"Thanks, Conon. That means a lot." She basked in the feel of her strong brother. The support of her family meant so much to her. She couldn't wait to present her mate to the pack.

He ruffled her hair just like when they were younger. She had been lucky to find her mate, but Conon was still searching for his special someone.

"One day I'm sure you will find your mate."

"I know she's out there somewhere. I'm patient enough to wait for fate to present her to me."

His smile didn't quite reach his eyes, and she didn't know which of their situations was worse.

"Zara!"

She looked up and caught sight of her father

strolling their way. He nodded to something behind them, and she turned around. Her breath escaped her while she stood to her feet. A small smile played out on her lips, and she took in the most beautiful sight.

Zara.

Zara's parents walked behind her, hesitant, taking in the wolves and humans mingling by the bonfire. It wasn't that often that a human came onto their pack's lands. Zara, of course, had been coming since they'd first met so it was second nature to her.

Marley's feet carried her over to her mate. She let loose a cry as they both ran for each other. She opened her arms, and Zara flew into them. Marley never wanted to let Zara go. Holding Zara immediately calmed her wolf.

"I missed you so much," Marley murmured against Zara's ear.

"I love you." Zara tightened her arms.

She released Zara, but they kept their arms around each other. Marley looked behind her to find her parents standing patiently by.

John and April stopped in front of them. Marley hesitated, unsure of what Zara's parents' reaction would be. At the hospital, it hadn't seemed as if Mr. York had taken too kindly to his daughter being missing. After speaking with her father, she understood what he'd gone through.

"Marley, I owe you an apology—"

"No, you don't," she cut him off. She glanced down at Zara and squeezed her shoulder. She was ecstatic to have her mate with her again.

"Let the man speak, Marley," her father murmured from behind her.

His strong hand patted her shoulder, and her body relaxed. Her wolf paced inside her chest, wanting to steal Zara away.

"I do owe one to you and your family," John stated, glancing between Marley and her family. "I wasn't thinking and I was an ass at the hospital. There was just so much going on in my head at the time, but that doesn't excuse my actions. We've had a long discussion with our daughter, and I am truly sorry. Please forgive me."

"John, we understood what you were going through. With the girls missing, it ripped our hearts out not being able to locate them." Her father moved to her side and offered his hand to Zara's father. "All is forgiven."

Tears filled Marley's eyes while she watched their fathers shake hands. Their mothers moved to each other and hugged, both with tears running down their faces.

"Let's go have a drink and give the girls some privacy," Jena suggested.

Their parents waved to them before walking toward the party.

"I told them everything," Zara announced softly, turning to her.

Marley's heart skipped a beat as she took in her mate.

"And?" she asked, searching for Zara's hand. She entwined their fingers, not wanting to let her go.

"They understand everything and that you are my everything." Zara sniffled, her eyes filled with tears. She wiped them away, a smile spreading across her face. "I don't want to be apart from you ever again. Today was too long, and I just want to be with you."

Marley's wolf howled. She pushed forward, wanting to be free, but Marley resisted. It was not time for her wolf to come forward. This conversation was for two humans.

Two women who were in love with each other.

Marley drew Zara completely into her embrace. She brushed Zara's blonde strands from her face and took in her beautiful smile. Her lips spread into a wide grin, knowing that this was the start to their forever.

"I missed you, too, mate. My wolf has been going crazy without you." She leaned her head down and rested it against Zara's forehead. She closed her eyes and breathed in deeply, taking in her mate's fresh scent.

She came back to me.

"Well, I hope you and your wolf are ready for me. Forever is a long time."

Marley opened her eyes and met Zara's beautiful ones. Forever sounded wonderful to her.

"I think we can handle forever with you." She bent forward and pressed her lips against Zara's. Her core clenched with the soft feel of Zara's lips. It had been too long since she'd had her mate.

"You think they will miss us?" Zara chuckled, pulling back slightly.

"I don't care if they do. Let's go home, mate," Marley growled, her lips brushing Zara's.

"I like the sound of that," Zara murmured, reaching up and entwining her fingers together behind Marley's neck.

Their breasts were crushed between them, and Marley wanted to feel Zara's body slide along hers with no barriers. A glint appeared in Zara's eyes while she slowly rubbed herself against Marley, and her wolf rumbled deep in her chest.

"Take me to your cabin, Marley. Let's go start forever now."

"Yes, mate. Anything you wish."

Zara sat back from her computer with a smile. She had just typed the magical words The End. She was impressed with her most recent book. Ever since they had got settled after returning home, a story had been burning in the back of her mind, and she knew her readers were going to love reading this story that was based off her true-life events.

Sailing with Her Wolf.

The past few months since she'd officially moved into Marley's cabin had been magical. She couldn't imagine life without her mate. Life with Marley was perfect. The pack had accepted her, and Zara loved living on pack land. It was just as Zara had told her family. Shifters accepted same-sex mating without a second thought, and they made her feel as if she had always been a part of the pack even though she was human.

Lately, Zara couldn't stop smiling.

She stood from her desk and closed her laptop. She'd been up since early morning when Marley had left to go for a run in her wolf form. Zara glanced down at her watch and left her office. Later, their families were going to be stopping by for dinner, and they needed to start preparing everything.

"She should be back by now," she muttered. She pulled the ties on her robe tight as she walked through their home. Ever since she'd moved in with Marley, they had made Marley's cabin *their* cabin. Marley wanted her to feel that it was her home, too, and they'd redecorated so that it was a home that displayed both their personalities.

She stopped in the kitchen by the back double doors and stared out at the beautiful land. She scanned the back yard, and her gaze landed on a black wolf lying near the edge of the woods.

Marley.

Her wolf was relaxing and taking in the warm sunrays.

Zara slid open the door and stepped out on the deck. Marley's head turned in her direction, and their eyes met. Her wolf's personality was similar to

Marley's, and if Zara didn't know any better, her wolf was grinning.

"Good morning, mate," Zara called out. She walked down the few stairs and sat on the second to last one.

Marley stood from where she was sitting and began walking toward Zara.

"You've been in your wolf form all morning. I want to see Marley now."

Marley froze and cocked her head to the side. Zara rolled her eyes, feeling playful. She knew Marley's wolf was taking offense that she didn't want her around but wanted the human side of Marley instead. Marley pawed the ground and released a snort.

"Don't make me beg to see my human Marley." Zara sighed. A grin spread across her lips. She knew how she could force Marley to shift into her human form. She moved her fingers to the ties of her plush robe. The ties fell to the side, and Zara pulled her robe apart, revealing her naked form. She ran her hands along her body and spread her legs, teasing Marley. Her head fell back, and she closed her eyes as she slid her fingers between her slick labia. A moan slipped from her lips while she dipped her finger into her warm core. She knew it wouldn't take long for her release to come, so she hoped Marley would make it.

"You know you don't play fair, right?" Marley's voice sounded in front of her.

Zara opened her eyes and found her mate kneeling before her. Marley's eyes crinkled in the corners with merriment.

"Your wolf can be as stubborn as you can be. I may not be an alpha wolf to be able to make you shift, but I have other ways to get you to do it." Zara spread her labia wide, showcasing her swollen clit.

Marley's eyes darkened whilst she glanced down at Zara's core. Zara moaned, loving the way her mate always looked at her. She massaged her clit slowly, teasing them both.

"What time is our family supposed to be showing up?" Marley asked, moving close to Zara. She leaned down and captured Zara's breast between her lips. Zara gasped, thrusting her chest toward her mate. She gripped Marley's head with her free hand, anchoring her where she was. Marley's talented tongue teased her nipple, and Zara cried out. Marley dragged her sharp canines across her nipple, and Zara whimpered, barely able to form a coherent thought to answer the question.

"Around five," she replied.

"Good, we have plenty of time for what I have planned for you."

Marley winked at her, and Zara leaned back against the stairs, offering herself to her mate.

"Have your way with me, mate."

<hr />

Loved this story? Check out Ariel Marie's sexy Moon Shifter Valley collection.
Download it HERE now!

A LETTER FROM THE AUTHOR

Dear Reader,

Thank you for taking the time to read my book! I hope that you enjoyed reading it as much as I enjoyed writing it. Please feel free to leave a review to let me know your thoughts. I love reading reviews from my readers. Even if you didn't like it, I would love to know why. Reviews can be left on the platform you purchased the book, and even Goodreads!

Love,
Ariel Marie

MOON VALLEY SHIFTERS

A FF Wolf Shifter Boxset

Three steamy stories of female shifters finding the mate destined for them. If you love sexy as sin, F/F wolf shifters paranormal romance stories, that will leave you breathless, then grab this hot box set!

Book 1 Lyric's Mate

Lyric moved to Moon Valley for a fresh start. A new town, a new home, and a new job was a dream come true. Finding that her new boss was her mate was totally unexpected. Will she be able to keep her wolf at bay?

MOON VALLEY SHIFTERS

Book 2 Meadow's Mate

Meadow, the new teacher in town had her eyes on the only female enforcer in the pack. Little did she know, the enforcer had Meadow in her sights. When a group of rogue wolves blows into town, will Sage be able to save her?

Book 3 Tuesday's Mate

Tuesday, the new accountant in town was setting up her new business in Moon Valley. Tuesday is entranced by Sunni, the coffee shop owner. Their wolves know they are meant for each other. But will Sunni and Tuesday listen to their beasts?

WARNING: These stories are sexy, fast-paced and will leave you begging for more.

Want to hear more from this tantalizing book? Download it HERE now!

ABOUT THE AUTHOR

Ariel Marie is an author who loves the paranormal, action and hot steamy romance. She combines all three in each and every one of her stories. For as long as she can remember, she has loved vampires, shifters and every creature you can think of. This even rolls over into her favorite movies. She loves a good action packed thriller! Throw a touch of the supernatural world in it and she's hooked!

She grew up in Cleveland, Ohio where she currently resides with her husband and three beautiful children.

For more information:
www.thearielmarie.com

ALSO BY ARIEL MARIE

Blackclaw Alphas (Reverse Harem Series)

Fate of Four

Bearing Her Fate (TBD)

The Midnight Coven Brand

Forever Desired

Wicked Shadows

Tempted by Fae Anthology Box Set

Paranormal Erotic Box Sets

Vampire Destiny (An Erotic Vampire Box Set)

Moon Valley Shifters Box Set (F/F Shifters)

The Dragon Curse Series (Ménage MFF Erotic Series)

The Dark Shadows Series

Princess

Toma

Phaelyn

Teague

Adrian

Nicu

Made in the USA
Columbia, SC
07 November 2024